Blurred

The Limit: I

Marissa Farrar

S.R. Jones

CASTLE VIEW
PRESS

Copyright © 2022 by Marissa Farrar and S R Jones.
All rights reserved.

No portion of this book may be reproduced in any form without written permission from the publisher or author, except as permitted by copyright law.

Cover Photo by FuriousFotog Cover by Marissa Farrar
Edited by Lori Whitwam
Proofread by Jessica Fraser
Published by Castle View Press

Authors' Note

Dear reader,

If you happen to know either of the authors of this book in real life, please don't mention that you've read it in front of anyone who might ask what it's about. We would like to avoid any red faces—both ours and theirs—when we attempt to explain primal kink!

Blurred Limits, as its title suggests, treads carefully around what may or may not be considered consensual. It also contains an extremely large, pierced 'eggplant', size kink, somnophilia, remote-controlled toys, and a character who tends to get a little too handsy around the throat.

But if you're into depraved men who want to chase an innocent girl who still has her V-card around an island, then this is definitely the book for you. If, however, you're reading this with your mouth open in horror, please, continue no further.

Happy reading!

Marissa Farrar and S.R. Jones

P.S. If you'd like a super smutty retelling of one of the scenes from the guy's POVs, then grab it here and sign up to Marissa and Skye's newsletters at the same time!

https://BookHip.com/DAGCKZV

Prologue

On the wall of security monitors, the footage of a girl running through the undergrowth was multiplied over and over. Her arms pinwheeled to keep her balance, and she glanced over her shoulder at something behind, her eyes wide with fear.

The high-quality cameras showed every detail—the scratch across her cheek where a bramble must have caught her, the leaf trapped in the wild knots of her blonde hair, the dirt on her knees and palms from where she'd fallen a little while ago.

Though, from inside the underground observation room, the four men watching were unable to hear, it was clear she was breathing hard. Her pulse must have been racing, her heart thudding, as adrenaline shot through her veins. She would be experiencing excitement and terror in equally arousing amounts.

The young woman was currently battling her way between tall palm trees and through lush green ferns and bushes, but the twelve miles of island wasn't all covered in foliage. One part was made up of sandy white beaches, while the other side gave way to cliffs, the ocean crashing against the craggy walls. The weather was mild right now, but it could turn, lashing the island with fierce winds and towering waves.

"Where are the hunters?" Rafferty asked, jerking his square jaw at the screens.

The youngest of the group, Asher, stepped forward and clicked the mouse, so the monitors flicked between various cameras. He pushed his black framed glasses higher up his nose. "There's one."

A shot of a man dressed in hunting gear appeared. He moved swiftly, but carried no gun. That wasn't what this was about.

"They've separated," Rafferty observed.

A gruff voice came from behind them.

"They're surrounding her," Wilder said. "Making sure there's nowhere she can run to."

Even though she'd run as hard as she could, the men chasing her were bigger, faster, stronger. They knew the island in a way she hadn't been allowed to. The fact was, there was nowhere she could run *to*. Nowhere she could really escape unless she planned on taking a long swim across a cold ocean. This was all an illusion, just like everything else. She'd been given a head start, but in the end, it wouldn't make any difference. They'd catch her eventually.

Asher chuckled. "They'll have their fun then."

Brody, the fourth owner of the island retreat called *The Limit*, raised his dark blond eyebrows. "So will she. It's not like she doesn't know exactly what's coming. She signed up for this. She read the waiver."

The four men turned their attention back to the screens. They'd split the view now, showing footage from different parts of the island. Their main focus remained on the girl, however, and she took pride of place in the center of the monitors.

One strap of her black tank top had slipped from her shoulder, exposing the top of one of her bra-less breasts. If it went much lower, she'd be flashing a nipple or two for them all to see. Not that she would have cared much about that. She had far bigger things to worry about.

"Where are the other two?" Brody asked, planting a hand against the wall beside him so he could lean against it. The ID tags—sometimes known as dog tags—from his days in the military hung across the front of his t-shirt.

Asher continued to flick through the monitors. The island was covered in tiny, secreted cameras that no one would spot unless they were searching of them. The size of the island made it hard to pinpoint their guests' locations, but Asher was an expert in knowing how these things worked, and he could normally narrow down an approximate location fairly quickly.

"There's one," Asher said, still focused on the monitors—computers were his thing. "He's ahead of her. She's going to run right into him if she's not careful."

On one of the monitors, the girl stumbled and fell. When she got up, her right breast was hanging out of her top.

Wilder's tongue snuck out and dragged across his lower lip. "Fuck, I'm getting hard just watching this."

"Down, Wilder." Rafferty smirked, adjusting the cuffs of his suit jacket. "This one's not for us."

Brody dragged his hand through his dirty-blond hair. "We'll have our turn soon, though, won't we? Our very own subject to play with."

Wilder smirked. "Won't be long now until we shut the whole resort down for our own game."

Rafferty rubbed his hands together. "Feels like it's been forever. You think this one will make it?"

Wilder snorted. "Nah, they never fucking make it. Even with the amount of cash up for grabs, they always bail. They think they know what they're getting into, but even when we've explained it in the most minute detail and they've signed to say they understand, they never really do."

"You think they're just blinded by the money?" Asher glanced over his shoulder at the other three.

"Maybe." Wilder rubbed at the tattoos scrawled up his thick neck. "I think most just have no idea how fucking depraved we can be."

A low rumble of laughter rose among them.

What they were watching on screen now was a toned-down version of the game they liked to play—a more palatable version. Even these men—and women—who thought they wanted to test their own boundaries really had no idea what limits could be reached.

"Look," Asher said, and jerked his chin at the screen.

A man stepped out from the undergrowth and caught the girl from behind, lifting her off her feet. Her lips parted in a scream, and she bicycled her legs in the air. His hand covered her bared breast, pinching her nipple hard enough that she froze.

"She's not fighting," Wilder observed. "They won't be happy if she doesn't fight."

Asher's brown eyes narrowed. "Oh, she will. She knows what part she has to play in this, and she has the safeword. If she wants it to stop, it will."

When the male guests signed up for this, there was one agreement that had to be made to ensure their cooperation if told to stop.

It wasn't about money—the type of people who came here wouldn't even miss millions. It was about reputation. They had to offer up one piece of information that could ruin them. It was the only thing they cared about and the one thing that would force them to play by the rules.

On screen, a second man stepped into shot. The girl kicked out, and he grappled at her feet. They were bare and couldn't do much damage, but it was clear her struggles excited him. He managed to grab her ankles in one of his hands, and he reached forward and tore her tank top, exposing her tits completely. Her nipples were dark, hard buds, and both men covered her body with their hands, squeezing and twisting. Her eyes slipped shut, her lips parting, the back of her head falling onto the shoulder of the man behind her. She was clearly enjoying herself.

A third man stepped out of the bushes and strode toward the threesome. Without pausing, he shoved the man in front away and then slapped the girl hard across the face. Her eyes sprang open, her jaw dropping in shock.

In the underground surveillance room, the tension in the air ratcheted up a notch. Blood pumped through veins, cocks grew harder, breaths became hoarse.

The men on screen threw the girl to the ground. She twisted onto her stomach and tried to crawl away, but one of the men caught her around the calf and dragged her back again. She fought back, but it was all an act.

Wilder caught his long, wavy hair up in his fist and exhaled a steady breath. "Fuck. I can't wait for our own hunt to start."

Rafferty removed his suit jacket and rolled up the sleeves of his shirt. "Be patient. We just have to wait for the right girl."

"I'm getting impatient." Brody cracked his neck. "How long is it going to take this time?"

Asher turned from the scene on the monitors. "We'll have one soon, and then the games can begin."

Chapter One
Honor

I SUCK IN A BREATH and approach the small seaplane waiting to take me across to the island from the mainland here in California, so I can start my new employment.

It's an easy job, and isolated, which is even better. Mystery surrounds the island where I'll be both living and working. I've tried to do some research about the place, but other than it being an exclusive retreat off the coast of Santa Barbara, I can't find much. It certainly isn't the sort of vacation you can book online, and I take that as a positive thing.

Despite meeting my employers later today for the first time, I haven't made much effort. It's become part of who I am to disguise my curves in baggy tops and to let my dark hair hang limp around my face. It's my curtain, my hideaway. Who knows what kind of steps *he* might take to find me?

It plays on my mind constantly. Has he hired a private detective to have someone follow me and take photographs of me? While a part of me wonders if he'd risk getting another person involved after what he did, the other part of me believes he doesn't give a fuck about someone else finding out.

I tear my thoughts from the reason I'm taking this job, and focus on what lies ahead.

I hope my being two days early isn't going to be a problem. It's a live-in job, and I was assured that the room was ready and waiting for me. The truth is, I'm all out of money and options. I've spent the last couple of nights sleeping on floors of train stations and bus shelters, and I'm not sure I can handle another night feeling vulnerable and exposed.

I mentally shake my head at myself. Who the hell am I trying to kid? I've always felt vulnerable and exposed, or at least I have been since my stepfather came into my life.

I've done my best to ensure I'm at least clean, washing in the sinks of public bathrooms and drying my clothes under the hand driers. It's not been easy, however, and I hope my appearance won't put my employers off. I've been assured that I'll have a uniform, which I'll be expected to wear when working, so I can put the baggy t-shirts away until bedtime.

Bed. The thought of sinking into a real mattress fills me with bliss. How long has it been since I last slept in my own bed? It must be almost two months now. I've lost track of time. What money I had burned away fast. I'd no choice but to purchase a burner phone, despite the cost. I did consider going without a phone altogether but knew I couldn't make that work in the long run. Without access to the internet, I wouldn't have been able to apply for this job.

An older, scruffy looking man—in his fifties, at least—climbs out of the cockpit of the plane and walks up the jetty to meet me.

"Name?" he barks.

He has a tablet in one hand—an iPad or something similar.

"Honor," I tell him, giving him my real first name. Though it's unusual, I think it's a risk worth taking. I don't want to make anyone suspicious of me because I accidentally forget to respond to a fake name or write down the wrong one. The surname, however, is fake. "Honor Harper." I bite my lower lip. "Sorry, I'm here early. I hope that's okay."

He frowns down at the screen as he plugs in my name. It must be difficult to see in the glare of the sunlight.

"You've brought your papers with you?" he demands.

"Yes, I did."

I'd already been informed that they'd expect to see my ID once I'd arrived. It made me nervous, but the one thing I do have is fake papers. It was a massive expense I could have done without, but what choice did I have? I knew the minute I tried to check into a motel under my real name, *he* would have found me.

The pilot holds out his hand for the real thing, and I dig into my bag.

My heart pounds as I pass them over. Will he be able to tell they are fake?

I need this job more than I've ever needed anything.

He scans my papers briefly. He seems impatient. He presses a few buttons on the screen of the tablet and hands the papers back. "Now you're in the system. Good to go."

I breathe another sigh. "Thanks."

I join him as we walk toward the plane. There's an image on the side of it—that of an eye inside a triangle. It looks familiar, and I wonder what it means.

The pilot side-eyes me and glances up and down. "I have to say, you don't look like their usual type."

I frown. "I'm sorry."

He glances away. "Never mind." He sniffs. "None of my business, anyway. Where's your luggage?"

I shrug the shoulder my backpack hangs off. "This is it."

I have my worldly belongings in this bag. That my life has amounted to this fills me with sadness. I remembered being younger and thinking my future was filled with endless possibilities, but gradually everything disintegrated around me, until I'd been left with no choice but to run.

I've never been on a plane like this—one where it takes off and lands on water. It looks cumbersome and like it will never get in the air. I picture us crash landing into water and squeeze my eyes shut, trying to dispel the image.

"What are you waiting for?" This guy needs a chill pill. No patience at all.

The plane moves beneath me, rising and falling with the water beneath it, and I clutch tightly to the open doorway, worried I'll slip and fall. I climb into the passenger side—there are only two seats in the whole plane—and look for the belt. The pilot hands me a headset, and I slip the headphones over my ears. Within seconds, the propellor starts up in a whirl of noise and movement.

Then we're moving across the water, leaving the mainland behind us, and as our speed increases, the nose lifts and suddenly we're in the sky. I squeeze my hands into fists and try not to look down.

To disguise my nerves, I ask questions. "How many times a day do you go between the island and mainland?"

His voice comes back to me through the headset.

"Only when I'm notified that someone needs to be picked up."

"Do people travel back and forth much?"

He takes his focus off flying plane and narrows his eyes at me. "Why all the questions?"

I shrug and glance out of the window. "Just making conversation."

Truthfully, I do have a reason for wanting to know. A higher turnover of guests means more opportunity for the man I'm running from to get onto the island. The thought that I might stumble across him one day while cleaning rooms fills my veins with a flood of ice. That this place is exclusive and difficult to reach brings me some peace, but I know I'll never be able to relax completely. I'll forever be watching my back.

It feels like only a matter of minutes have passed before we're losing altitude again. Ahead, a large island rises out of the water. The ocean, tipped in white waves, surrounds it. As we get closer, I make out a dock with a white, expensive-looking boat moored, and out of the greenery rises a huge building made of concrete, glass and steel. The sunlight reflects off all the glass and catches another plane of light—a swimming pool. There's no doubt in my mind that this is where I'm going to be working.

To my surprise, a flicker of excitement ignites inside me. I might only be cleaning, and it isn't as though I'll be allowed to use any of the facilities, but there are definitely worse places I could be.

We touch down on the water, and I brace as we lightly bounce across the surface. The sea is relatively calm, and I don't want to think about what this must be like in rougher water.

Our speed decreases, and soon we're coasting along, just as though we're in a small boat, and the pilot navigates to the dock.

It's a bit wobbly as I climb out onto the jetty, and, once more, I picture myself slipping and falling in, but I make it onto dry land without making a fool of myself.

A small, two-seater, soft-top Jeep is waiting for me. From the air, the resort hadn't appeared to be far from the dock, but now I have my feet on the ground, I can tell it's a good distance—probably farther than would be comfortable to travel by foot. Besides, it doesn't look as though that's how things are done here.

A second man is driving. He's younger than the pilot, and dressed almost entirely in khaki. I'm reminded of a tour guide on a safari. Perhaps that's his role here—to guide people around the island. I wonder how many staff they have here, and who I'm going to meet. I'd love to find a friend again. It feels like I've been alone for such a long time.

The sun heats my shoulders and the top of my head, and I'm grateful to escape into something with air conditioning. Without waiting for an invitation, I open the passenger door. He doesn't even look at me, but starts the engine.

"I've been instructed to take you directly to meet the bosses," he says.

Bosses? Plural?

That was new to me. I always thought there was only one person at the top.

"Oh, of course."

I suddenly find myself wishing I'd made a little more of an effort with my appearance.

The resort is set on the highest point of the island, and the road winds between palm trees as we climb toward it. The windows are open, and the breeze carries on it the scent of the ocean and something floral too. Birds flutter from branch to branch, their song filling the air. It combines with the buzz of insects and the distant crash of waves upon the shore.

I'm apprehensive about meeting my new boss—bosses—but then I'm apprehensive about pretty much everything these days. I must admit this beautiful setting helps to ease my fears. Just being in this location feels good for the soul.

As I'd expected, my driver doesn't take me to the front entrance of the resort, but instead takes me around the back to what must be the staff entrance. He parks, and we both jump out.

"This way," he says, marching off so I have little choice but to follow.

I notice he hasn't asked anything about me—not even my name—but I guess he doesn't see it as being his business.

It's cool inside the building, a welcome change from the heat of the sun. Though, from the outside, it looked to be more glass than concrete, I find myself following the driver through a whole heap of windowless back passages. I assume these are for staff only, and out of bounds for the guests. We catch an elevator up a couple of floors, and then step out onto a far plusher looking corridor. The carpet is thick and bouncy, the walls hung with expensive looking artwork.

The driver stops at a set of double doors. He knocks once, and then tells me to go through.

Anxious about what I'll find, I open the doors and step into a huge half-moon shaped room. Floor to ceiling windows make up the entirety of the curved wall, offering an incredible view of the island and the ocean beyond.

But the beauty of the room I find myself in isn't the thing that captures my attention.

Four men dominate the space.

The men are all different in appearance, but each has an air of authority about him. I'm sure, once this meeting is done, they'll expect me to be neither seen nor heard. Men like this didn't deal with domestic staff. I'm actually a little surprised they wanted to meet me in person. I'd expected the housekeeper who'd set up my employment to be the one to run me through everything.

A man with black hair and bright blues eyes is the smartest dressed of them all, and he picks up a tablet and swipes his finger across the screen.

"Honor," he says, apparently reading it from the tablet. "Honor Harper. That's your name?"

I nod. "Yes, sir. It is."

Something flickers across his features when I call him sir.

"Thank you for coming."

Instinctively, I'm drawn toward the man who is closest to me in age—early to mid-twenties. He wears a pair of black framed glasses, a set of warm brown eyes behind them. A tattoo crawls up under the short sleeve of his white shirt, but I can't quite make out what it is.

"You're aware you need to sign the waiver?" the suited man asks.

BLURRED LIMITS

It's part of the contract that I'm not allowed to speak about this place. No posts to social media. No photographs allowed to be taken. Not even chatting about it to friends—not that I have any friends. It makes me wonder what kind of thing goes on here, but I discover that I don't really care. Being safely off the mainland and having a roof over my head is enough to make me agree to pretty much anything.

I nod and stare at the floor, unsure where to look.

One of the men completely overshadows the room. How can he not at his height? I'm guessing he's at least six feet four. But that isn't the only thing that makes me battle with myself not to stare. He's covered in tats—hands, neck, basically every piece of skin except for his face. The silver glint of a ring is in his nose. His hair is as long as mine, light brown waves—and underneath it is shaved close to his skull in an undercut. He's thick with muscles, bulked out beneath a form-fitting gray t-shirt and light blue jeans with holes in them. He wouldn't have looked out of place in a Viking movie.

Do they own this place, or just manage it? The vibe I'm getting from them is that they're alpha males and they won't have anyone above them, but that seems like an unusual setup.

The suited man studies me intently. "Good. And there's nothing you want to add or take away?"

I'm not sure what he means. "Like what?"

"Nothing you won't do?"

I bite my lower lip. "If it means I can stay here, I'll do anything you tell me."

This seems to please him more than I'd intended, and a flush of heat rises up my chest, over my neck, and condenses in my cheeks. I sense the gazes of the other men on me as well.

The fourth of the men looks like a grown-up version of the jocks who picked on me in high school. Tan with longish, scruffy blond hair. Dimples when he smiles—which he's doing, but not in a friendly way, more like he's thinking about what cruel things he can do to me. I shake the thought from my head. I'm being paranoid. I'm here to clean rooms and change beds, that's all. And, dressed as I am, with a face free from makeup, I'm fairly confident that I'm not the sort of girl a man like him is interested in. I imagine his girlfriend—assuming he has one, or perhaps he has more than one—would be nothing like me. I shoot a glance to the other men. Or maybe a boyfriend? If he has a girlfriend, she'll be five feet ten, blonde as well, with big tits and tiny designer clothes. I'm tiny, at only five-two, and while I have curves, they certainly don't look like anything beneath my baggy t-shirt. But then that's the point of wearing it.

"That's what we like to hear." Suit purses his lips, his gaze raking up and down my clothes. "You can't wear that."

"Oh, no. I wasn't expecting to."

"Good."

He must have pressed some kind of buzzer, or sent a message, as a knock comes at the door, and then a woman enters. She's in her sixties, I guess, and is tall and bone thin. I feel even shorter than normal, which isn't helped by the massive man with the long hair who is behind me.

"I have a new one for you, Felicity," he says. "Work your magic."

She ducks her head in a nod and cocks two fingers to beckon me toward her.

I realize I've been dismissed.

"We'll see you soon, Honor," the suited man calls after me.

There is something I don't understand in his tone. As I walk away, a tingle of goosebumps rises across my skin.

Chapter Two
Honor

I FOLLOW FELICITY AS she click-clacks down the corridor on her high heels. Those red soles tell me her shoes cost more than my entire wardrobe.

Being a housekeeper here obviously pays well. So does this maid's job, which is why I need it. Which is why I will not freak out at the weird setup here. Weird, I can handle. Being found by *him* again, I cannot.

Felicity turns right, and I almost bump into her as she stops by an elevator. We enter it, and it heads down. Of course it does. Up is where all the gorgeous rooms will be. The views of the ocean and beyond is what money will buy.

VIPs go up...the hired help goes down.

The doors swoosh smoothly open, and Felicity leads me down another endless corridor, though this one has glass on one side. We're on the ground floor here, but the way the building is built right into the hillside means the other side of this floor was built into the rock. I glance out of the window and can't see much. There are plants, lots of them, and trees, and not much more of a view. Still, the greenery is lovely, and if this is the view from whatever tiny box-room I'll probably be calling home, it's a damn sight better than the bus terminal.

Felicity reaches a door at the end of the corridor, punches in a code, and opens it, ushering me in with a sweep of one long arm.

I head inside and stop, almost tripping over my own feet.

What the hell?

The space is cavernous.

This room is as big as a house. Huge bay windows look out over more greenery, and tantalizingly, through the trees, glimpses of blue. The ocean.

There's a sectional sofa facing a mammoth television with what looks like one of those fancy sound boxes underneath it. Snaking around one side of the room is a bar, and it's fully stocked. I don't understand. I thought I'd at least be given the chance to change and settle in before they put me to work.

"I—I thought I'd need to change before I started."

She shoots me a look, her brow furrowed. "That's what you're here to do."

"Change? In here? Shouldn't I go to my room first?" I start to wonder if I've made a mistake. "This is a live-in job?"

"Of course," she snaps. "This is your room."

My jaw drops. "It's more..." I search for the right word... "opulent than I was expecting."

Felicity turns her cool gaze my way. "Don't get used to it. You won't be spending much time in here."

I suppose not. The hours *are* long. The job did also specify that overtime will be expected. For what they're paying me, I can work sixteen hours a day if they wish. I'm young and healthy, and I need the cash. I so badly, *desperately* need the cash.

"Now, obviously, you need to clean up." She raises one arched brow and looks down her nose at me.

I flush and want to hide from her disdainful scrutiny. *You try to keep clean in the bus station bathroom*, I want to say. Of course, I can't, so I clamp my mouth shut, biting the inside of my cheek until it stings.

"Although one might argue that you've already piqued their interest more than any of the others. Can't tell what you've got hiding under those baggy clothes." She smirks.

"What?"

She ignores me and continues, "You need to bathe. Now. There are strict rules in place for personal hygiene on the island. I'll go through it all with you, but you need to be clean, shaven, and scented."

"Excuse me?" This gets weirder and weirder. What the hell have I gotten myself into?

Rich people and their foibles. I remember my auntie's words from a long time ago. She used to work for the super-rich as a maid. The things she'd tell me, never naming names, of course, were crazy. They'd request that she only clean with filtered water and that carpets needed to be vacuumed in a certain direction. She'd even gone in one time and been made to throw away hundreds of dollars' worth of perfectly good food because the client had thought there was a strange smell coming from the refrigerator. But yeah, the rich are weird, and if I have to shave my legs to earn my paycheck, so be it. To be honest, after the last couple of weeks, it will be amazing to pamper myself.

"This way."

Felicity leads me into a bathroom, and I gasp. No way. No frickin' way. I wish I could call my bestie, Ruth. She'd go nuts if she saw this. I can't risk it. I don't want to put her in any kind of danger. Speaking of. I rummage in my bag and take my phone out. No signal. Weirdly, that makes me feel more secure. Despite it being a burner, I'm still paranoid about *him* finding me.

"You're not allowed to use your phone on the island," she says. "No photos either. There is a landline phone in your room. You may use that if you need to make a call."

I shove my phone back in my bag and continue my awed appraisal of the bathroom.

The floor and three of the walls are marble, for God's sake. The other 'wall' is a huge floor to ceiling window, with the free-standing tub right in front of it.

"Erm, it's stunning, but won't people be able to see me bathe?"

Felicity looks at me as if I'm stupid. "It's one-way glass."

Of course it is.

Marble shelves line the wall to the left of the tub and hold glass bottles from brands I don't know. Oh, Hermes, I recognize that one. Wow.

"Get undressed, then," Felicity snaps.

With her in the room?

She turns the taps, and water cascades into the huge tub.

"I'll fill the bath for you and then leave you be. What scent would you like to use? I suggest picking one and sticking with it."

"Erm, I don't know."

She leans in and sniffs me like a dog. I flinch, and it takes all I can not to move.

"I'd suggest something darkly sensual, but with a hint of fresh. Not grapefruit, though. Maybe a fig-based freshness. Woody rather than citrus. Yes, fig, layered with something complex. Or if not fig, something woody, but layered with vanilla, and some musk. Rose?"

I'm staring at her, completely lost. This is really weird. They want their maids to wear a signature scent? Who cares what the room cleaner smells like?

"I know." She takes a bottle from the shelf. It's unmarked, a deep amber liquid in heavy, cut glass.

The bottle is wafted under my nose, and I blink at her in surprise. "What is that scent?" It's the nicest perfume I've ever come across.

She shrugs. "It's custom-made. *Ange et Demon*. Angel and Demon." She chuckles, and the sound is so cold it sends shivers up my spine. "Perfect for you, little one, with your dark hair and pale skin and those big eyes, but with the sense and planning to hide all you have under these baggy layers. Already playing the game, huh?"

"Game?"

She glances at her watch. "Take your clothes off, please. You need to get washed. You can't possibly stay like this..." Her hands wave over me as if to indicate the horror of my unclean self.

"Okay, okay." Shamed, I rush to get undressed. Felicity doesn't even glance my way, and she's a woman, I tell myself as I try not to feel shy. She's probably done this lots of time with the new hires.

"Right, your bath is ready." She bustles into another room and comes out with a basket in her hands a few minutes later. "Shampoo, conditioner, and hair oil in the same scent. Body lotion. Soap. A wet razor and a dry battery razor. Also, one of those epilator things, but I always find them excruciating."

"I can use the normal razor to shave my legs, thank you."

"And your armpits, and between your legs."

I'm about to step into the bath and almost fall in at her last words. I wobble and hold on to the side.

"I beg your pardon?" Oh, this is too much. I can't subject myself to this humiliation. Not even for the pay they're offering. "It's no one's business what I do with my lady bits but mine."

"Shave it, or leave." She purses her lips. "It's the rules."

"What kind of rules are they?"

"*Their* rules. Their island. Their resort. I only do my job."

I can't help but bristle. "Ah, the 'just carrying out orders' defense."

I clamp my mouth shut. I don't mean to back-chat her, but this is nuts. I close my eyes briefly and remind myself how much I need this job. I can go back to being broke and sleeping on the street, or I can do what's being asked of me.

"I'm merely asking you to shave yourself. It's hardly harmful. Now, these dramatics are becoming tiresome. Do you wish me to tell the gentlemen you've changed your mind, and get you on a plane back to the mainland? I can do so right now."

I stare at her. She's a coldhearted bitch. It's written all over her face. Then it hits me. This is probably some sort of hazing ritual. This evening, when I sit with all the other staff, they'll have a good laugh that I thought I really had to shave my lady bits to keep the job. But, right now, if I don't, she really might tell the men to send me back, and I can't have that. She's right. It's only a shave. What does it matter? I also don't want her to think she intimidates me.

I laugh, as if this is all silly fun. "You're right. I normally shave anyway. This is a nice luxury after...erm... roughing it in my last job."

Damn it, Honor, nearly slipped up there and let her know you've been sleeping in bus stations.

She narrows her eyes but merely nods. "Good. Press that buzzer on the wall when you're done. I shall bring you some clothes. There are towels in the cabinet at the far end of the room. Grab one before you get in."

Then she's gone, closing the door behind her.

I'm relieved to be alone.

Naked, and feeling all kinds of shaken up, I pad across the room. Halfway to the cabinet, I pause. The floor is the perfect temperature. It's not cold like marble should be, but it doesn't feel heated. I bend down and press my palm against it. Perfect, like the air on a summer day. Control freaks, the lot of them. I huff out an annoyed breath and grab a towel. Then I head back to the bath. To one side of it, in a recess of more marble, is a walk-in shower. It contains a large, square head, but also what look like jets from the sides too. Maybe next time I have a wash, I'll try it.

As I sink into the bath, all my worries and questions fade away.

The water is heavenly, the bath so deep I can lie right back with the water lapping at my chin, every part of me covered.

The scent the housekeeper chose for me wraps itself around me in the steam. It's decadent, sexy, but not cloying. I look out of the window and watch the small palms blow in the gentle breeze.

This is heaven.

I feel like Cinderella taken from her life of desperation and poverty and whisked away into one of opulence. But perhaps I'm more like Beauty, trapped with a beast, or rather four of them. Despite my pleasure at the bath and the luxury of the room, I can't shake the feeling that something is very off here.

I splash my hands in the water and sigh. As my dear mom liked to say, if it seems too good to be true, it probably is. God, I miss her. I push her out of my mind because missing her hurts too much.

After ten minutes of letting the heat unknot my tense muscles, I pick up the soap and thoroughly wash myself. Then I take the razor and shave my legs, armpits, and finally, my pussy. As I do so, for some reason, I imagine the man with the glasses and the kind eyes watching me. I felt an instant connection with him in that room. The others were all too scary in their own way, but he seemed nice. Hot, too. I like nerdy guys.

Most women would have gone for the Henry Cavill lookalike, or maybe the Viking, but not me. Give me a geek any day.

Climbing out of the bath, I pat myself dry with the softest, fluffiest towel known to man. It's like drying myself with a cloud. Then I apply the scented lotion over every inch of skin. I wrap the towel around my hair, grab another from the cupboard for my body, then press the buzzer.

The door opens five minutes later, and Felicity walks back in. She's got a bundle of clothes in her hands.

"Much better," she states with a crisp smile. "Drop the towel and let me look at you."

I do as she says, and immediately curse myself. Why did I do that? This isn't normal. Sometimes, I have this deep-seated urge to obey, to do as I'm told so I don't have to think, and it's screwed up. I've spent so long left pretty much to my own devices and making decisions for myself, from far too young an age, that I think I've got an authority complex. Some sort of submissive streak.

Certainly so, if my fantasies are anything to go by. Not wanting to think sexual thoughts while this frigid woman appraises me like a slab of meat, I push those away.

"Good. These are your underthings."

Underthings? She sounds positively Victorian. The underwear she hands me is anything but. A black silk thong, with a matching silk bra. I've never owned real silk before. I consider protesting, but frankly, the panties I've been washing in bathroom sinks for the past couple of weeks have seen better days. I move quickly, wanting to have at least something covering me—no matter how small—and as I pull the thong on, it caresses my skin, making me shiver.

I suppose they choose this stuff so as not to show under the maid's uniform.

"Don't put the rest on just yet," Felicity barks. "Let me sort your hair."

She marches over to me, pulls the towel from my hair, and dries it roughly. She's hard enough with her movements I wince.

"This way." She leads me back across the bathroom to where the towels are kept and opens a second cupboard, where she takes out a drier. She styles my hair with the drier and a big paddle brush, and when it's done, she grabs a silk scrunchie and pulls my hair up high, securing it in a swinging ponytail.

I'm starting to feel a little better now. This is more normal. A ponytail, to keep my hair out of the way when I'm cleaning. Underwear with no lines for underneath the uniform.

"Okay, your clothes."

She passes the bundle to me, and I start to sort through them. "There must be some mistake?"

"Why?"

"This is what you want me to wear?"

The trousers are black, and as I pull them on, yep, as tight as I thought looking at them. They're not denim, but a sort of thick cotton, stretchy, denim-like material. Tight, and tapered at the ankles, they leave little to the imagination and seem somewhat casual for a maid's uniform.

I put the top on next. It's a ribbed tank-style top and as tight as the trousers. Also in black.

"There's a sweater too, in case you get cold. Shoes, you have a choice of the ankle boots, or the black sneakers. You'll be on your feet a lot, of course. Cover a lot of miles. You need to be comfortable."

I suppose I will cover a lot of miles. This is a huge resort, and I hadn't thought of it that way, but to clean it will mean walking its length and breadth regularly.

I pull the ankle boots on, and she smiles.

"Finishing touch." She takes out a small pouch from the bag slung across her body. Then she applies a red tint to my lips.

She stares at me for a long moment, her scrutiny unnerving. "So naturally pretty, you hardly need any enhancement. They're going to love you." She walks to the door. "Come. I will go over the rules with you in the staff kitchen. You can have something to eat and drink. You'll need your energy."

I follow her out of the bathroom and through the opulent living space. As I do, I catch sight of myself in a full-length mirror. Holy hell, the clothes are tight. They're sexy but in a strangely utilitarian way. I almost look like I might be about to go fight in some underground war.

"This is a strange uniform," I mutter.

"And yet so practical for what's to come." Felicity grins, sugary sweet and fake, as she opens the door.

My heart drops. What *is* to come?

Chapter Three
Honor

I FOLLOW FELICITY THROUGH the warren of corridors. I'm so going to get lost daily.

She leads me into a large professional kitchen that's all shiny stainless steel but is strangely deserted. There are no chefs in whites rushing around, shouting to one another as they prepare meals. It occurs to me that though I've met a couple of the staff, I haven't actually seen any guests yet.

"Where is everyone?" I ask. "I thought there would be more people here."

"Not yet," she replies. "The owners like to use this...period...to get the place up to scratch for the next influx of guests. The standard of people we have here means that everything has to be perfect. They don't expect anything less."

"No, of course not." I'll have to make sure I deliver on their high expectations. "How many guests do you have here at any one time."

There's a reason behind my questioning. I want to know how likely it is that my stepfather will be able to make it onto the resort, if he were to find me.

"Only a handful. These people like to have their own space, and they pay enough for it."

"Of course." I hope that means I'll be safe. My stepfather has ways of getting what he wants, but even he might find it difficult to get here.

"Would you like a tea or a coffee, or will you join me in a glass of white wine?"

It's early in the day for drinking, but I'm on edge, nervy, and the day has been extremely strange. Plus, I haven't had a glass of wine in months. It sounds lovely.

"Wine, please."

"Good."

The way she speaks is ever so slightly European. The crisp manner she bites off her consonants makes me wonder if she's German or somewhere Slavic.

"Take a seat," she orders.

I do as she says and hike myself onto one of the stools placed around a large steel worktop. This is where Felicity placed her bag, so I presume it is where we are sitting.

Glancing at her bag as she fills two glasses, I let out a little gasp. "Hermes? Your work bag is Hermes?" I'm confused at how someone of her position can afford such things. "You're the housekeeper, no?"

She lets out a huffed laugh, handing me a glass of wine. "No, I'm not. The housekeeper, Olivia, is currently unwell. She's picked up a vomiting bug, so will be kept isolated for at least the next few days. The last thing we need is something like that running through the resort. I'm the gentlemen's personal assistant, which means I run this place, effectively. Or at least, I run the details. The small things. My employers like everything to operate smoothly, which is where I come in. The big decisions, they make, of course."

"I see."

I find myself relaxing at this piece of information. That explains a lot. No wonder she's been so strange with me. This isn't even her role. She's probably pissed that she's been landed with me and was taking out her frustration by seeing how far she could push me.

"Drink," she orders.

Does this woman say anything without it coming across as a demand?

I do as she says and sip at the wine. God, it is delicious. "Lovely," I say.

"Gewurztraminer." She smiles her cold smile. "The best white wine in the world, in my opinion. It's from Alsace."

It is by far the nicest wine I've ever tasted. The cool, slightly sweet liquid dances on my tongue. There's not the usual hint of vinegar that I'd get in the cheap wines I used to drink with Ruth.

The alcohol warms my stomach, and I begin to feel more than a little fuzzy headed. I realize I've been guzzling it. I've not slept properly for days, and eaten very little. I slow my roll and push the glass away slightly. "Do you think I might have a tiny bite of something to eat? A glass of water, too?"

"As soon as we've got the rest of the paperwork out of the way, yes."

"More paperwork?"

God, I'm so tired. I want to rest for a few hours. My shifts weren't supposed to start for two days. I'd hoped it would have given me time to sleep, eat, and get some stamina back.

I'm pretty fit and was a champion at track, but the endless months of sofa surfing, cheap motels, and outright rough sleeping have taken a toll.

She frowns at me. "This is the really important part. What you're here for, no? The money."

I return her frown. My wage is already agreed. I open my mouth to say something, but she takes two pieces of paper out her Hermes bag and pushes them my way with her blood-red nails.

I glance at them, then stare. One is for...no this can't be right. One is for two hundred thousand dollars, and the other, oh, my God. I feel faint.

The second check is for a million dollars.

Two things hit me at once as I sway on the stool. Firstly, there's been a mistake somewhere along the way here. I'm not sure what this is, but I'm pretty sure none of it is meant for me.

Secondly, that million dollars would mean freedom for me. Freedom from *him*. Nothing else matters. It's life or death for me. He knows that I know the truth, and if he finds me, I am dead. This job was to be nothing more than a reprieve. Now, it's become a chance for true freedom.

"Why the difference?"

She sighs. "Oh, now, don't play coy. You know why. What you might not know is that not one single woman, not one, has ever walked away with the million." She gives an elegant shrug. "But it's not as if two hundred thousand is anything to turn your nose up at, right?"

It isn't. Even that amount will buy me a heck of a lot of time. I could survive for years on it. But survival isn't the only thing I want. I want to reveal the truth about the man who's destroyed my life. I want people to see him for the monster he really is, but I can't do that on my own. I'd need to employ the same kind of people he's probably hired to find me. To do that, I'd need the million.

"And to get the million, I only need to..."

"Finish the game. By finishing, lasting it out, you win the ultimate prize."

"The game?"

"Yes, *their* game."

She means those four men. Suddenly, things start clicking into place. The way they looked at me. Their surprise at my attire. The bath, the...oh, Lord, the shaving myself.

They think I'm someone else.

Shit. What kind of *game* is this? I know it must be something sexual—depraved, even.

My stomach turns sour. Talk about out of the frying pan and into the fire. I'm running from depravity; why would I even consider placing myself firmly into it?

Because this is different. This is controlled. This is four hot-as-hell men. You ran from him because he's disgusting, vile, and cruel, but these men?

I close my mind to my inner voice and try to keep calm. Decisions made from a place of panic are always bad decisions.

Felicity pushes what appears to be a contract under my nose. "Now, are you going to sign it or not? You can still walk away if you choose to."

"No, I—" I pull the paperwork toward me and pick up the pen.

"Get on with it, then. We're already late," Felicity says. "To be honest, I thought you were going to be a no-show. It's happened before. They get cold feet."

She's just answered my other worry. I thought if the person they thought I was showed up, then I'd be in deep shit. But the other woman isn't here, and she's late, which means she's likely not coming, for whatever reason. In two days, they'll realize the maid didn't show, but so what? They won't care about a maid, and simply hire someone else.

I stare at the contract, eyes scanning the words, which swim in front of me. If I do this, I can change things. I can start a new life, and more importantly, I'll have money available to start an investigation of my own. I have no idea how that kind of thing works, but with enough cash behind me, I'm sure I can figure it out, or at least I can pay someone else to figure it out.

"You need to remember the safeword." Felicity taps a section of the contract with her finger. "Ragnarök. Don't forget it, whatever you do. It'll make everything stop if you really can't bear what's happening."

But I wonder what happens if I use the safeword.

She seems to read my thoughts.

"You drop out, you get the two hundred thousand, and you go home. No harm, no foul. You manage to be the first woman to hold out, though? You're a millionaire."

"So I understand fully, the safeword means it all ends, right? No in between. There's no...minor safeword? For if something goes too far, and I want that to stop but not to end the entire game?"

"It's all or nothing. You say the word and it all ends. You take your two hundred K, and you walk. You don't say it, all bets are off. You have no control other than that word."

This is insane.

I've fallen down the rabbit hole, but that amount of money leaves me reeling. I cannot walk away from this once in a lifetime chance. So what if four men want to play perverted games with me? I can do this. I'm stronger than I ever thought possible. The past two years have proven that beyond a shadow of a doubt.

I suck in a breath and sign the contract in my fake name. Honor Harper.

"Ragnarök." I pick up my glass, take a huge gulp of the wine. "Ragnarök. Ragnarök." I emblazon the word on my brain.

Felicity stands. "You ready to play?"

My insides churn like they're on a spin cycle, but I nod. This woman is going to hunt me down herself when she realizes she just offered the maid the chance to win a million dollars, but that's her mistake, not mine.

Chapter Four
Rafferty

THE TENSION RADIATING from the others is palatable.

Wilder paces, his hands knotted in his long hair.

Asher sits at his laptop, his fingers running over the keys as he tries to distract himself with something online.

Brody throws a tennis ball at the wall, catching it each time it rebounds to him, before throwing it again. The steady *thunk-thunk* of the ball hitting the wall isn't doing anything to help relieve the pressure in the room.

Everyone wants to get on with the game, but we need to give Felicity time to run our little rabbit through the rules. And show her the money. It's one thing knowing that kind of sum is up for offer, but it's something else to see an actual check with a million dollars on it. It makes it real.

Just like with the finances that made buying the island and building the resort possible, the payment comes from my money. Not that I give a shit about it. Even the million-dollar check is a mere drop in the ocean of my inheritance. Money has become irrelevant to me.

Each of us brings our own set of skills and talents to the table. Sometimes, I wonder if mine is the least important, or at least the thing that says the least about me. Anyone can have money. It's so fucking superficial. Maybe that's why I've donated so much to the others, so I can feel I'm actually making a difference to people.

Wilder is our survival expert and allows us to give our business a legitimate cover by running survival experiences for businesspeople come the winter months. Brody spent years in the army, has fought for our country and seen and experienced things I don't even want to think about. It's affected him—not that he'd admit it—but we each have our scars. That's the thing that brought us all together. The other thing that brought us together was Asher. Without him and his ability to work the dark net as though he lives there, we might never have known of each other's existence and our shared pasts.

Our ultimate goal is what we live and breathe, but there's nothing wrong with a little entertainment while we get everything in place.

"What did you make of her?" I address all three of them, wanting all their thoughts.

Wilder stops pacing. "She seems different."

"I thought the same. What the fuck was going on with her clothes?"

Normally, girls showed up here dressed like they were about to go to a strip club. Short skirts. High heels. Tops that barely covered their tits. This one—Honor—had turned up in baggy jeans and a t-shirt. Her hair looked like it needed a good wash, and she hadn't had a scrap of makeup on her face.

To be fair, what Honor had been wearing was far more suitable for what lay ahead than the fuck-me heels and faces covered in makeup that we normally saw.

BLURRED LIMITS

Brody catches his tennis ball and doesn't throw it again. "Perhaps she just thought it would be more practical."

"The type of girls we normally get here tend not to give a fuck about practical," I point out. "They want money and some fun and games, until they realize the fun is too hardcore for them."

Maybe she lied to us and the only reason she's here is for the money. Most women come here for a combination of both, but she might have her eye on the prize and *only* the prize, and that's the main reason she's here, rather than it being about sex.

Brody snorts. "Not all of them care about the money. We've had rich women happy to come here for a good week of being fucked by multiple men. They know they're not going to get an opportunity like this again."

Wilder cracks his tattooed knuckles. "Well, none of them have made it to the million yet."

"That's hardly surprising after what we put them through," Brody says.

I purse my lips. "She just seems different. It's not just the clothes. She seems...innocent."

Asher spins in his seat, and his brown eyes glint with a fresh kind of darkness. "Maybe she is. She's young, after all. Hell of a lot younger than you or Wilder. Maybe that's a virgin pussy we're about to get our hands on."

I roll my eyes. "Don't be an idiot, Ash. It doesn't suit you. There's no way a virgin would put themselves forward for this."

He pouts and wheels back around to his laptop. "Can't blame a guy for dreaming. I'd love to wreck an innocent little cunt."

"As long as it isn't Wilder who does it." Brody chuckles. "Then there'd be nothing left for the rest of us."

It's no secret among us that Wilder isn't lacking in the massive cock area. It's hardly surprising—the man is built like a fucking giant. That he also has a penchant for tiny women also isn't a secret.

"Let's just see how she gets on with the first game," I say. "For all we know, she'll tap out the moment this all becomes real to her."

Brody drags his hand through his scruff of blond hair. "I don't know. There was something about her, something tough. She might look innocent, but I got the impression she might have been through some shit."

I cock an eyebrow. "You got all that from spending five minutes with her?"

He shrugs. "Needed to be able to read people quickly in my previous line of work. Maybe I'm wrong. I guess we'll find out soon enough."

I check my Rolex. "Felicity should be done with her soon."

As though my words have summonsed her, a knock comes at the door. We all exchange knowing glances, the atmosphere in the room almost crackling with anticipation.

"Come," I bark.

The door opens, but only by a foot or so, and Felicity slips her whip-like body around the gap.

"She's ready for you, sirs."

A frission of excitement goes through me. "Bring her in."

Felicity glances over her shoulder and gives Honor—who is still in the hallway and just out of view—a nod. She opens the door wider and allows Honor to step through, before retreating and closing the door behind her, leaving us alone with our new girl.

Fuck me.

Honor looks incredible in the clothes we've provided for her. Her long, silky hair—which is tied up in a high ponytail, perfect for us to grab if needed—is almost as dark as her black, skin-tight outfit. I can make out every curve—the generous swell of her chest, the almost impossibly tiny waist. I could probably get both of my hands around her and touch my fingers together. An image jumps into my head from one of the games if we catch her. Her seeing how long she can take us spanking her before she uses the safeword. It's not only her ass we'll smack, either. Our handprints will be all over that pale skin—on her ass and her tits. We'll get her to spread her legs so we can smack her bare pussy, too.

Her gaze darts between us nervously.

"Turn around," I instruct her. "Let us see what our money has paid for."

She looks as though she's thinking about refusing, but then she turns in a slow circle, her hands in fists by her sides.

I nod approvingly, and from the reactions of the others—a grunt of appreciation from Wilder, a flick of his tongue across his lower lip from Brody, and a hand squeezing his dick from Asher—I can tell they feel the same way.

Oh, yes, a tight ass, but still big enough to want to smack so we can watch it jiggle. Her pale skin contrasts to both her hair and clothes. She has a red tint on her plump lips, and it makes me want to cover her mouth with mine. She really is quite lovely.

I move closer, and the scent that Felicity has provided her with fills my nostrils. She smells incredible. It's all I can do to prevent myself running my nose up the side of her throat and breathing her in.

"Do you know my name?" I ask her. We use pseudonyms when messaging our potential playthings, and I don't know if Felicity has filled her in on who we are and how to address us.

She doesn't meet my eye but shakes her head. "No."

"No, sir," I correct her. "My name is Rafferty. You don't need to know my surname."

"Should I call you Rafferty, or sir?" she asks.

I pick up on a hint of mockery in her tone.

"That'll depend on the situation. In formal situations, such as this one, it'll be sir. In less...proper...circumstances, you can scream my name."

Her eyes widen.

I hold back a smirk and step back to allow the others time to introduce themselves.

Wilder steps into her personal space, and she rears back. It's a normal reaction. Most people would feel intimidated having him close. It's not only the size of him, but the body that's almost completely covered in tattoos. I wonder what Honor will make of his pierced nipples and cock.

He runs the back of one of his fingers down her cheeks. "Dark hair, pale skin, red lips. You're like a real-life version of Snow White."

"You don't seem like someone who's into fairytales," she shoots back. "Unless you're the ogre under the bridge."

I find myself wanting to applaud her snark. Not many people would dare to talk back to Wilder.

He leans in closer. "I guess we'll find out how much of an ogre I am, Snow. You can call me Wilder."

She shoots a look to Asher that screams 'help me.' Women often make that mistake. With his glasses and slighter build, Ash looks like someone people can trust. But the truth is, Ash is the reason we all came together in the first place. He's into all kinds of shady shit on the dark web, and he's the one out of all of us who I genuinely fear will take things too far one day. Luckily, he's got us around him to make sure that doesn't happen.

There is only one person we have ever wanted dead, and it definitely isn't one of our guests, whether they be hunter or prey.

Chapter Four
Honor

I'M SO NERVOUS, MY knees are literally shaking. I'm doing my best to hide it beneath my bravado, but I don't think I'm fooling anyone. I feel nauseated and as though I'm detached from the room, but I know that's the adrenaline. Though I was in a room with these men earlier, something feels like it's changed. They're predatory now, and I have no doubt that I'm the prey.

The man I'd recklessly called an ogre has stepped back, and the younger one who'd been sitting in front of an expensive looking laptop rises.

"I'm Asher," he tells me. "Or you can call me Ash."

"Not sir?" I check.

A smile I can't quite read crosses his lips. "Sir works for me as well."

Like the big, tattooed man has done only moment before, he lifts his hand to my face. But it's not my cheek he touches. Instead, he runs his fingertips down the side of my neck.

To my shock, he suddenly wraps his hand around my throat. I draw in a sharp breath. Perhaps I should yank away, but instead I freeze. I expect him to tighten his grip, to close off my airways, but he doesn't. His hold is firm, but not punishing. It's more like he's measuring me for size.

From behind Asher, I hear Rafferty's warning tone. "Asher..."

Asher releases me, and I dare to breathe again.

"Good." He nods. "Very good."

My mind is spinning. I don't know what to think. He hasn't hurt me, but I felt as though he was trying to warn me about what he's capable of.

The only one who hasn't approached me yet is the blond.

I don't know for sure, but from looking at them, I'm guessing at least two of these men are significantly older than my twenty-one years. The one they call Wilder I'm guessing to be in his mid-thirties. A fifteen-year age difference is something I've never thought about before, but I find it intimidating. I'm guessing Rafferty is also in his thirties, but blondie seems younger—late twenties, perhaps.

Blondie doesn't bother to approach me, but props himself up against the wall behind him, his arms folded, one ankle hooked around the other.

"Are you tattooed anywhere?" he asks. "Pierced?"

"No."

"Virgin skin." He smirks. "I'll look forward to putting our mark on it."

His words alarm me, but I remind myself of the money, and the fact that I have the ultimate say here. These men are scary, but whatever they are doing is in a strange way controlled, with a very clear out for me if I need it. That out, strangely, gives me the confidence to feel as if I can do this. Like a safety valve. Just knowing it is there is reassuring.

BLURRED LIMITS 51

"What—what do you want me to call you?" My voice shakes, and I hate how it sounds.

"I'm Brody. You can call me that."

With introductions done, I look around the group. I'm thirsty for knowledge, while simultaneously not wanting to know.

"I—I don't really understand what I'm supposed to be doing?"

Rafferty takes over the conversation again. "You read all our communications, no?"

"Umm...yes," I lie. "But it was a while ago now."

He eyes me curiously. "Not that long ago."

"Sorry. I've had a lot going on."

I wonder if he'll ask me exactly what I've had going on, and for a moment, I wonder if I'll tell him. The story sits on the tip of my tongue, ready to spill from my mouth. It would be like a purge, finally confiding in another person about my fear and suspicions. It feels like such a long time since I had someone on my side. I haven't even been able to confide my fears to Ruth. I know what she'll say—that I need to go to the police—but how can I when he *is* the police? Everyone respects him, and I'll just be looked at as the troublemaker who wants to take out her grief and anger on an innocent bystander. Also, if I tell Ruth, I worry that it will put her in danger. She's far safer not knowing

The younger one, Asher, steps in, and though I'm grateful to him for it, I can still feel the imprint of his fingers around my throat.

"That's okay," he says. "We'll run through the rules of each hunt before it begins."

I swallow. "Hunt?"

The corner of his lips twitch, but the expression doesn't reach his brown eyes. "Or call it a game, if you wish."

It dawns on me that I'm going to be the prey in this 'hunt,' and the game they want to play is me. My stomach churns with a fresh bout of nerves.

Rafferty steps in again.

"Here's how it works. Since there are four of us and only one of you, and we know the island and you don't, you'll get thirty minutes head start. I suggest you put as much distance between us and yourself as you can in that time."

I'm starting to understand the outfit. Yes, it's sexy, in a kind of Lara Croft way, but it's also practical. The material is thick, but stretchy, the boots low heeled and flexible. It'll allow me to move with ease.

"Where am I going?"

He hands me a piece of paper, and I glance down to see it's a map.

He grins. "X marks the spot."

"That's where I'm supposed to get to?"

"Each day, there's an item you need to find. It's in the place marked on the map. If you reach the spot and find the item before we catch you, you win, and you'll get to come back to your room. You can take a bath, and order room service—drink champagne and eat chocolate covered strawberries, if you so choose. But if we catch you first, you're ours, and we get to do whatever we want to you."

I swallow. "Whatever you want?"

"Whatever we want," Rafferty echoes. "There are five days and five hunts. Each day, it'll get harder. The run will be more dangerous, the challenge harder, the things we'll do to you when we catch you will get..." —he pauses as he searches for the right word — "more intense."

"Don't worry," Brody says, "we'll ease you in slowly. Today isn't the official start, today is a little bit of fun—for all of us, hopefully—so you get the idea and have a basic understanding of the concept. After today, all bets are off."

Wilder gives me a wolfish grin. "Or you could just not let us catch you."

Unable to keep it in any longer, I blurt, "I—I'm a virgin."

Oh, crap, why did I say that?

Asher lifts both eyebrows. "You're joking, right?"

My face burns. "No. Why would I joke about that?"

Rafferty takes a step toward me. "You sign up to play this game with us, and then you tell us you're a virgin? Is that supposed to make us take it easy on you?"

"She thinks if we do," Brody says, "it'll be easier for her to win the million."

Rafferty cocks his head to one side. "Is that right? You're trying to play games with us? It doesn't work that way, sweetheart."

That hadn't been my intention at all, but I can tell by the cold glint in his eye that no amount of pleading my case is going to work. I am in way over my head here. A part of me wants to use the safeword already—Ragnarök—but the image of the million-dollar check remains clear in my mind.

After everything I've been through over these past few months, I feel like nothing these men can do to me can be any worse.

"I'm not trying to play games. That's your job." I still need to get some things straight in my mind. "If you catch me and I can't do what you're asking of me..."

He preempts what I'm asking. "Then you use the safeword, and it stops. But if you use the safeword, the game also ends. You'll be handed your check for two hundred grand and leave the island."

It occurs to me that this could be the easiest two hundred grand I ever earn, and if I didn't need substantially more to be truly safe, I could safeword out early in the proceedings.

"Don't you worry that women will sign up for this and just use the safeword right away and take the money?"

Rafferty frowns. "Why would they do that?"

"Well, to get the money, of course."

He stares at me, and I feel like he's stripping me away, layer by layer, trying to see exactly what is beneath. "Because this isn't just about the money, is it? It's about the chase, and the catch. It's about knowing what it's like to have four men track you down and for you to run and fight them and for them to take you anyway. You know, it's your fantasy. Too. We discussed this."

My voice is tiny. "Oh, yes, of course. It just seems more real, I suppose."

Rafferty hasn't finished. "It's about returning to our basest state. People will argue that we've evolved now, and we have, but that doesn't change how that little part of our primal urges still exists. Thousands of years ago, women chose their men based on who was the biggest and strongest, and most likely to protect and provide for them and pass on their good genetics to their offspring. And men would take their women by force, literally dragging them to their caves by their hair and taking them whether they wanted it or not. Now, we have evolved, and plenty of people would say they no longer had any connection to that part of themselves, but those of us who admit it want a safe way to experience those fantasies."

I gulp. My skin feels like it's on fire. My nipples have hardened beneath my tank top, and I wonder if they're visible to the men. Rafferty's gaze drops, and his smirk tells me he, at least, has noticed.

I'm building a picture of what I'm taking on. They're going to hunt me across the island, and if they catch me, they'll do what they want to me. But if I beat them and make it to the mysterious X and locate whatever the item is I'm supposed to find, I'll be safe, and I'll get to come back to the luxurious room, to the deep bath and the soft bed.

Untouched.

A shiver of something I don't quite understand courses through me. The tingle runs down through my body and settles in the form of heat between my thighs. I've had those thoughts, haven't I? When it's been late at night and I've been unable to sleep, I've slipped my hand between my thighs and fantasized. In my imagination, some gorgeous but dangerous man has broken into my house and finds me upstairs in bed. I'd try to run, to dart for the bedroom door, but of course he'd block the way. I pictured him catching me around the waist and throwing me to the bed, where he'd pin me down and tear the clothes from my body. It never took long after reaching that point for me to find my orgasm. I never considered for a second that it was something I'd actually want to experience in real life—the prospect would be terrifying and damaging—but in a fantasy it was controlled and safe.

Only now these men were offering to make a variation on that fantasy come true, and it didn't feel controlled or safe in the slightest. Yes, they'd given me a safeword, but where was the certainty that they'd even listen if I used it? We were out in the middle of nowhere, with no one other than their staff on the island, and I could scream that safeword from the top of my lungs. It didn't mean they'd listen.

No, this is too much. I haven't had one man, never mind four of them, and it isn't as though these men are the gentle, loving, tender type either. They literally want to hunt me across a private island.

Just don't let them catch you.

It really is as simple as that. There are five days, five hunts, five challenges, all starting tomorrow with a little taster game right now. I might be able to make it through each of them without the men ever laying a finger on me. Then they'll hand me a check for a million dollars, and I'll be set for life. I can use the money to get proof about what *he* did and put the man chasing me away for life.

Now I know I'm dreaming. That's never going to happen. The best I can hope for is vanishing and creating a new life for myself. It sours my stomach that *he'll* get away with what he's done, and that everyone will continue to believe he's some upstanding member of society when that couldn't be further from the truth, but what can I do?

I straighten my shoulders and lift my chin. I hate that I haven't had a proper sleep in forever, or a decent meal, and that puts me at a disadvantage. I'm not as strong as I'd like to be. I'm tempted to see if they'll let me start tomorrow, but I can already tell from the hunger in their eyes and the tension in the room that they can't wait to get started.

"Okay, I'm ready. We can start the hunt."

Chapter Five
Wilder

RAFFERTY GIVES HONOR the map and talks her through what she needs to do. Today isn't a big deal. It's a small chase, and one we always win, so we can ease them into it with something light, set their minds at rest some, give a false sense of security before the real fun starts.

There are two reasons for it. One, we want them to rest tonight, and if they haven't started the games at all, they won't sleep. Too churned up and worried, and excited with fear of the unknown.

Secondly, we want them primed, turned on, for when the real games begin. This is about the push and pull of them wanting it, but not wanting it. We're fucking careful when we talk to the women we choose, and that's why all my spidey senses are tingling that something is off with this woman.

She seems *too* nervous. *Too* unsure, and the virgin shit...? She did *not* mention that in any of our online chats. Maybe the others are right in thinking it's her way of us making things easier on her. *She* could be the one playing games with *us*, which isn't how things normally go.

Rafferty hands her the small backpack with the water in it, a snack, the map, a compass, a light sweater, and a fold-up poncho, just in case.

"Go," he tells her.

And then she's off out the door. Small, fragile, shooting us one last terrified glance before she leaves.

My dick is so hard it hurts. For my cock, this is perfect. Small. Scared. And apparently fucking untouched. My dream come true, but my mind is screaming at me this is wrong. She's wrong.

We watch her in silence on the monitor for a few seconds as she leaves the building and makes her way across the decking and through the vegetation toward the ocean. Great start; she's going the wrong way.

"I don't like it. I say we call this one off," Brody rumbles.

His words shock me because I was about to say something similar.

"No fucking way," Asher snarls. "She's perfect. Jesus Christ, I can't wait to get my hands on her. Have you seen how pale her skin is? She'll mark so prettily. And a virgin." He laughs. "Come on, we couldn't have produced a more perfect little morsel if we'd designed her ourselves."

"Yeah, exactly, genius. It's all a bit strange," Brody snaps. "I don't like it. What if she's a cop or a reporter?"

"What if she is?" Rafferty turns to the room from the monitors. "This isn't illegal, and she's signed the contract now. It doesn't matter what she finds out, she can't say a word about it. Not about this, not the shit we do when we let rich men reserve the island in the summer and do the exact same thing, and not the shit we do when we chase billionaires and give them a beating and a day's worth of light torture. They're all consenting adults. All safety waivers are signed. Yeah, we keep it quiet, on the down low because we don't want the publicity or the hassle. But if it comes down to it, we're golden. Legally, at least. In the court of public opinion...who knows? But do any of us care?"

"She's not a cop." Asher laughs. "No way. She's a naïve young woman, who has fantasies about being forced, who somehow found us on the dark web, and who now realizes the reality. She's in over her head, but she has the safeword. She can stop this right now. All she has to do is look at that camera and say the word, and she gets two hundred K for nothing."

"Yeah, and she might do that any second." I put in my own view. "So, why don't we save ourselves a couple of hundred grand and stop it now?"

"She still gets the money," Rafferty states. "It's in the legal small print. I take care of that so none of you have to, but she still gets the money."

"Okay, but we haven't done anything yet." I push my point farther. "If we stop it now, we aren't liable for any shit that might come our way. A *virgin*?"

"Oh, come on." Asher walks over to me, his dark eyes glinting with malevolent intelligence. "We all know your...predilection for tight pussies and tight bodies. She's going to be perfect for you. A dream come true."

My cock will destroy her pussy, and while the thought makes me even harder, it also gives me pause. Something about her made me feel protective. A feeling I've not had in the longest time.

"Look, I get it," Rafferty says. "She's not our usual type in many ways. Physically, yes, but not in the way she's acting. We normally get women who have been playing for a while. Know what they like and want the money. She's not like that. But the fact she's different makes it more entertaining. And at any point, she wants to stop, it stops." He snaps his fingers in the air. "She's ultimately got the controls here, boys. I say if she wants to carry on, who are we to stop her?"

"Seconded," Asher says immediately.

"I don't know." Brody runs his hands through his hair, mussing it even more. "Something about this doesn't sit right with me. She might fuck this up for us, if she's some sort of plant."

"We'll note your concerns," Asher says with heavy sarcasm.

"Two against two. You're not in charge here," I reply.

"If we stop it, we might be liable," Rafferty says.

"What?" I can't believe this.

"Yeah. I mean, she can stop it at any time. She has the control, the safeword. She entered into a legal contract with us, and it gives her the chance to win a million dollars. If we stop things now, she loses that chance. Could leave us open to legal action."

"Fuck." Brody sighs.

"Look," Rafferty says, "we're either all in, or we're out. We stop this and give her the two hundred thousand and hope she goes away quietly. Or we proceed as usual. She's an adult. She knows she can safeword, and *we* all know that each and every one of us would be a fucking liar if we said she isn't perfect for us."

She *is* perfect. I want to see those big, blue eyes widen as I push into her tight pussy for the first time. I want to see if she can take me, and how she'll handle my piercing. The thought almost has me coming in my pants.

"Okay," I say. "Fuck it. I'm in."

"Brody?" Ash stares.

"Yeah. Okay." He's still paranoid; I can hear it in his voice.

I have reservations, but right now, my little head is most definitely winning in the battle against my big head.

"She's not even looked at the map yet." Rafferty points to the screen.

Honor is on the beach. She opens her arms up and out and drops her head back. There's a beatific smile stretched across her face as the breeze plays with her ponytail. She looks so damn innocent and happy in this moment. Something tugs in my chest. Something I've not felt in the longest time.

"She needs to get a move on," Asher grumbles. "At this rate, we'll simply stroll up to her and grab her and game over."

"We all know what the plan is for this first time, yeah?" I ask.

"Yep. Catch, and release, with a bit of humiliation thrown in." Asher smirks. He likes the humiliation part.

"Get her all hot and bothered but don't give her any release." Brody starts to look less worried as he smiles.

"We normally let Wilder be the one who makes himself come while the target is being pleasured but maybe we ought to switch it up," Rafferty muses.

Oh, hell, no. My dick will burst. "Why?" I demand.

"Most of the women playing our games love your monster cock. We know it will turn them on, as well as scaring them a little bit, in the best way. This one? I think it might be a bit too much."

"Plus," Asher says with a dark laugh, "I want to see her face when she sees it for the first time further down the line on this and realizes what she's got to take. Why don't you get her to the edge, Rafferty, and Brody, you be the one to come on her?"

"No," Brody says. "Not doing it. That's not my role today. I hate it when we fuck up the order."

"We need to know you're all in," Ash pushes.

"Yes, we do," Rafferty says. "I agree. I'll play with her a little, until she's wet and desperate and half looking forward to tomorrow, as well as fearing it. You cum all over her and show her what her place is in all this. Total mindfuck."

"Nice little bit of humiliation kink." Asher chuckles.

"Christ, you're fucked up, you know that?" Brody shakes his head.

"Yeah, and you're a real choirboy."

"Enough." Rafferty asserts his unspoken position as the head of all this. We don't officially have a leader, but if Rafferty walks, we're finished because he supplies the money. "We carry on as normal. I accept full legal and financial responsibility if something goes wrong. No more arguing, okay? We need to be tight for this to work."

"Okay," I say.

"Yep." Brody nods.

"Ash?" Rafferty waits for a long beat.

"You've got it," Asher says.

Sometimes the age difference between him, myself, and Rafferty is stark. Guy's still almost a kid in some ways. Closer to Honor than he is us.

How someone so young got so twisted up is a whole story in itself.

I glance at the screen and see our little Snow is finally on the move. She has the map in hand and keeps glancing at it, and then around her. It seems she knows how to read it, which is an improvement on last year's plaything.

Gina.

I think back to her with a small smile. She'd been fun, but she couldn't read a map, had zero survival skills, and very little common sense. As a result, she got caught every time and tapped out on game four. Still, she almost made it. Rafferty gave her a hundred grand bonus for doing so well.

Terrible at survival, she'd been into the sex. It was the other stuff she'd balked at. Asher's stuff. Sick fuck. I throw him a glance. Sometimes, I want to punch him in the face. Then I remember why he's the way he is, and I feel badly for him.

I stare at the monitor and move in closer. Honor is inspecting a plant. It's edible, and when she takes a leaf, rubs it, sniffs it, and then takes a small bite, I smile. Clever girl.

Honor nods to herself, as if satisfied the plant is the one she suspected, and carries on her way.

I glance at my watch a while later. Thirty minutes. She's covered a hell of a lot of ground compared to most of the women we have here. She's fit, however. Petite in build, sure. Smaller than any other woman we've played with, but she's got smooth muscles under her skin, curves, and the way she moves is certain and surefooted. This isn't some trust fund baby who has spent her life in high heels and close-fitting gowns the way Gina was. She'd lost her trust by getting involved with a boy Daddy disapproved of, so for her the whole thing had been a way to get some money back, as well as a giant *fuck you* to her controlling father.

I wonder what Snow White's story is.

"It's been thirty minutes," Rafferty says.

My dick is hard as hell thinking about what we're going to do.

Snow is going to get an introduction to the reality of the games.

Chapter Six
Honor

I find the cave and smile. This will make a good hiding place for a few minutes while I catch my breath. I have no watch on me, so no way of knowing the time, but it feels as if I've been running a while now. I'm getting tired. I need a drink and maybe a snack.

This island is full of edible fruits and plants. Not surprising, as it's off the California coast and bathed in sunshine for much of the year.

It's slightly north of LA but not much. I was slowly working my way north, trying to get to the border eventually. Canada had been my only hope. Now, with the prize money, if I can win it, I can go anywhere.

Montenegro was the place I'd fantasized about reaching, and with the money, it would be in my grasp. In Europe, but not in the EU and with no extradition treaty with the United States, I could start over again there safely. It's also beautiful. With a million pounds, I could live a very happy life somewhere like that, and still ensure *he* gets what he deserves. Maybe even pursue my love of writing, though I haven't written a word since my mother died.

When I was a child, I used to think I'd write a book one day, but as I grew, I discovered my love was more with poetry.

Except, it wasn't poetry I was writing, but song lyrics. Before my life turned to shit, I even played around with singing what I'd written, strumming out a few chords on a guitar. But I'd never be brave enough to sing in front of anyone else. My dream is for a real artist to produce my work, but I don't kid myself into thinking that will ever happen.

I take my water out, sit down gratefully on the sandy interior of the cave, and drink. There's a protein bar in my bag, so I eat that, and then drink some more. I rummage around in the bag, exploring. There are a couple of snacks. A rain poncho. Water. Gum. A small Ziplock bag, which I open to find a couple of Band-Aids, hand sanitizer, cotton pads, some rubbing alcohol, and a lip balm. Oh, God, are those? Yep, condoms and a bottle of lube. I roll my eyes. How thoughtful.

Rubbing some of the balm on my lips, I drop it back in the bag and zip it closed. Then I take a piece of gum out and chew for a few minutes as I look at the map. The island is bigger than I'd first thought. Plenty of places to hide. They've got the advantage. They know this land, and probably are aware of every single hiding place on the island.

I wonder if they have cameras. I bet they do, the weirdo perverts. I snort a laugh, and then sober when I hear a noise. It's a crunching, like a branch breaking. Oh, no. No way could they have found me so fast.

Holding my breath, I creep toward the entrance of the cave. Male voices carry on the wind.

"Oh, Snow, we only want to play."

That's the big one, what's his name? *Wilder*. Yeah.

Crap. I don't want them to catch me, not on day one, but then...if I let them catch me today, I can gauge a better idea of what they're all about. Today is, how did they put it? *A warmup*. It might be in my best interests to let them think they won today.

After all, this way, I can get an idea of the kinds of games they'll be playing and maybe get into their heads a little. They think they have all the power here, but do they? In some ways, yes, but in others, I also have some. I'm what they want, after all. I saw the hunger in their eyes. I'm their prize. The thing they want to play with, and maybe break, but what if they can't break me?

What if I'm already broken beyond repair?

I bet they didn't think about that.

Deciding to see what I'm in for, I purposefully linger until I hear them come closer, and then I dart out of the cave and make a run for it.

"There, to the right," one of them shouts.

Heavy footsteps pounding behind me come closer and closer. I'm running as fast as I can now, weirdly enjoying the adrenaline rush that comes with being chased this way. A heavy weight plows into me, and I cry out as I go down. Bracing myself for pain, I breathe when none comes. Instead, the man taking me down the ground bears the impact himself as he rolls onto his back, holding me to protect me.

Interesting.

When he rolls us again, so I'm below him, I see it's Rafferty. I'm surprised. Any of the other three I'd have expected this from, but not Mr. Suit and Tie. Except he's not wearing them now. He's got a t-shirt covering his broad chest.

"We meet again," he says with a grin.

Then he stands and pulls me up. I scream as I'm swept off my feet and thrown over his shoulder like a sack of potatoes. He walks me back to the cave, where the others are, and the fear kicks in for real.

He's so powerful, and he's not even the biggest. Wilder is massive.

I'm so petite that any man is going to be stronger than I am, but three of these men are heavily muscled, and I don't stand a chance.

Terror surges in me, my heartrate kicking up as terror overwhelms me. What was I thinking? I'm going to find myself in a situation I can't get out of.

My hands ball into fists, as I prepare to fight or run as soon as Rafferty puts me down.

We enter the cave, and he slides me to the ground. The moment my feet hit terra firma, I feint to the right. Asher mirrors the move and gets in my way.

I try to go left, but there's Brody. He's wearing a baseball cap and has it pulled down low over his eyes.

At the entrance to the cave, anyway, like a sentinel standing guard, is Wilder.

Nowhere to go.

Nowhere to run.

Trapped.

My heart is pounding like a rabbit's. Beating against the prison of my ribcage as if it can escape and take flight itself.

"Nowhere to run to, Snow," Wilder says with a shake of his head.

"No need to be scared," Asher says. "This is an easy introduction, okay?"

BLURRED LIMITS

I swallow and step back but hit something solid and warm.

Big arms come around me, and I'm trapped in a warm cage of skin, muscle, and heat.

"So beautiful." Rafferty twists my hair in his fingers. I hold still as he lifts it to his face. I have my head slightly to the side, so I can't see him properly but can make out enough in my peripheral vision to see him take a sniff at my hair.

That's weird.

"Smells like heaven. It's the color of a raven's wing. So dark it shines almost blue."

I make eye contact with Asher, not quite as sure of him since he got hold of my throat, but still drawn to his warm gaze and his handsome but nerdy features.

"Don't look at me for help, baby girl. This one isn't my show."

"It's mine," Rafferty says with the hint of a low groan to his words as his hands skim down my sides. "I think we ought to see a tiny bit of what we've paid for. Don't you?" He whispers the words in my ear, but it is more than loud enough for the others to hear. "How about a game of truth or dare?"

I don't like the sound of this.

"Wilder, you go first." Rafferty is still stroking his hands down my sides and the backs of my arms. He's not touching me in an overtly sexual way, but with the other three men all watching every tiny touch with a raw hunger, his fingers burn on my skin.

"Okay. I pick truth." Wilder shrugs.

"What do you most want to do to your Snow here?"

He smiles, slow and lazy, and slightly one-sided. It changes his entire face, and suddenly I see how handsome he is. A fact

I'd not noticed because I hadn't looked beyond his ink and his size.

"I can't wait for her to wrap those lips around my cock. I'll feed it you nice and easy, baby," he says. "We'll go slow the first time."

My mouth is dry, and the erotic images his words create flash through my mind. My clit pulses against the tight fabric of my pants, and I drop my gaze to the floor, unable to hold Wilder's any longer.

"What about you, Ash?" Rafferty says. "Truth or dare?"

"Dare," he replies immediately.

"I dare you to show our girl here just how much you want her."

I expect him to take his clothes off, or pull his dick out, but Ash walks right up to me, and takes hold of my hand. He presses it against his hard, and surprisingly big, dick, holding it there for a moment.

My lips part as I breathe heavily.

He rubs my palm against his pants a few times, his hips moving in time to my touch.

"Soon, you'll learn exactly how I like it," he tells me, his voice gruffer than before.

"Do you want a turn yet?" Rafferty asks me.

I shake my head.

"Okay, my turn. I choose truth. Anyone want to ask me a question?"

"What's the most depraved thing you've done?" Asher asks.

Rafferty laughs, his breath blowing deliciously against my exposed nape. "Well, I don't know. I've done a lot of things.

I think possibly that time Wilder and I had a woman take us both in her pussy at the same time. Fucking insane."

"Christ, she came so hard. Soaked us both." Wilder grins.

Oh, God. I'm simultaneously horrified because two dicks in one pussy sounds so intense, and also unbearably turned on.

Rafferty moves his hand to cup my mound, and my breath stalls in my throat. He doesn't undress me, or do anything but put pressure right where I need it. It feels so good that for a moment I forget myself and let my head drop back onto his shoulder as a small moan escapes me.

"Good girl," he murmurs. "See, it's not scary, is it?"

"Her turn," Asher says. "What do you choose? Truth or dare?"

"Truth," I manage to pant out.

I open my eyes and look at the three men watching me like birds of prey watching a field mouse.

"When you're rubbing that virgin pussy at night, the way Rafferty is now, do you imagine some big, bad, faceless man pushing you down on the bed and taking your precious little cherry?"

Asher's words are so scarily close to my fantasies that I choke on my answer, unable to mortify myself by giving it.

"Truth, baby girl. You chose it. You don't give us the truth, and this won't be the gentle introduction we promised."

"Okay, yes. Yes, I do."

Rafferty moans in my ear and increases the pressure on my pussy. He's rubbing me through my clothes, but with the dirty talk and the men watching me, it's enough to have me almost coming. I can feel it building, and realize my hips are moving, pressing my core against his hand where I need his touch the most.

My lips part, the wave of pleasure starting to rise, and I still as I wait for that first rush of release to wash over me, when Rafferty takes his hand away.

A whimpered cry escapes my lips, and I turn around, but he's shaking his head. "Uh-oh, not the first time, sweetheart. You get your turn to come tomorrow, when the games start properly." Then he leans in close and tips my chin up, brushing his perfect lips softly over mine. "But only if we catch you."

He spins me back around so quickly, I feel dizzy. I'm facing the others again. "Want to see something of our little prize?" he asks them.

"Been waiting long enough." Brody steps out of the shadows. He hasn't spoken yet, and his dick is obscene in his sweatpants. He's hard, and there's no disguising it.

"Let's show these boys some of the goods, huh?"

Rafferty pulls my top up swiftly, exposing the skimpy silk bra, and pulls it over my head. He tucks the top into the back of his pants, making it clear I'm not getting it back any time soon.

"Goddamn, look at those tits." Asher moves forward. "Baby, how did a little thing like you grow those?"

I want to smack him. He's looking at me like I'm a lump of meat. Cocky. Sure of himself. He messes with my head. Such a nice face—kind, even—and the glasses, and the nerdy presentation, but then he comes out with shit like that.

He reaches out a hand, but Brody slaps it away. "No touching the goods, Ash. Not for you. Not today."

Rafferty slowly pulls the cups of the bra Felicity made me wear down on each side, so my breasts are pushed up, the

BLURRED LIMITS 75

material gathering under them and offering them for show to the men.

I'm ashamed, turned on, and wanting more, but I'm not sure what of.

"Beautiful," Brody murmurs. "How about I show you something in return?"

I swallow and don't move a muscle.

Slowly, he pushes down his sweats, revealing no underwear and a long, hard, cock.

He takes it in his hand and slowly runs his fingers over his length, smearing the pre-cum at his tip all the way down.

My mouth waters at the sight. He's perfect and unashamed.

"Look how hot you've got me," he says. Then he snaps his gaze up to Rafferty. "Get her to her knees."

Rafferty pushes me harshly to the ground. I stumble forward, my hands digging in the sand and my cheeks flushing as Asher's laughter follows me.

"Straighten up," Rafferty orders, pulling my shoulders up and back.

I'm kneeling in front of Brody now, like some sort of offering to him.

He moves closer, and I think he's going to make me suck him. Instead, he strokes the back of one knuckle down my cheek. He looks at me from under the brim of his baseball cap.

"Such a pretty girl." His gentle words are at odds with the fierce expression on his face.

Then he begins to move his fist up and down his length, thick veins ridging him. I watch, mesmerized. I can't stop myself. His fingers are wrapped perfectly around his girth as his movements pick up speed. I hear the clink of metal with his movements and realize he's wearing a chain of some kind beneath his t-shirt. I refocus on his cock. The head is darker than the rest of him, and more precum leaks from the slit. The scent of salty musk fills my nostrils, and I find myself inhaling deeper. The sense of shame I feel to be in this position only adds to my growing excitement.

"You love watching him working his big cock, don't you?" Rafferty says as he plays with my ponytail, wrapping it around his fist and tugging sharply so darts of pain spear through my scalp.

I nod because I do, and for some strange reason, in this moment, I can't seem to lie.

"Mark her, cum on her, show her who she belongs to," he orders Brody.

Brody grunts and jerks, and his cock erupts, covering first my breasts and then my face with jet after jet of hot cum.

I'm so shocked my mouth falls open, and he aims a spurt right in my mouth.

"Fuck," he says as he pants, his fist slowing. He squeezes one last, thick drop out of his cock, and then pushes it back into his pants.

I raise my hand to wipe my cheek, but Rafferty releases my hair to grab my wrist, stilling the movement. "Oh, no. You wear that all the way back to the compound. And you'll thank Brody now."

"*Thank* him?"

"Yes."

"For what?"

"For the gift he gave, and for not making you lick it clean."

BLURRED LIMITS

I shake my head. Suddenly my horniness is overwhelmed with sheer, white-hot anger. I won't thank him. They can go to hell.

"Say, '*Thank you, Brody, sir, for not making me lick it clean*,'" Rafferty orders.

"No."

"Excuse me?" Brody walks forward, and there's menace in his gaze. "You don't get to say no, Honor. That's not your place in this."

For some stupid reason, I feel tears threatening. "I...you...control," I blurt. "You said I had the ultimate control."

"Christ, didn't take her long," Ash sneers. "Thought she'd be tougher, got to admit."

What does he mean?

"You want to safeword out?" Wilder asks.

Do I? It's not the sexual side of things, it is the humiliation. I don't know if I can do it. And mostly, it's not the two men who've been doing stuff to me, either. It's the other two.

Wilder, watches me with an odd mix of tenderness and raw, wild hunger to match his name. That hunger of his terrifies me.

And then Asher. His cocky, arrogant smirk makes me want to do violence.

"You say the word, this all stops." Wilder nods at me once. "Listen to me, Snow. We will stop."

And just like that, I feel safer. I do have the control. For a tiny moment, Wilder broke the spell of the game and showed me the human side of himself, and the truth. If I say Ragnarök, they will put an end to this.

Asher snorts at Wilder and shakes his head.

"I don't want to stop," I say. Then I lift my gaze to Brody and swallow the thick reluctance coating my throat. "Thank you, Brody, sir, for not making me lick it clean."

"You're welcome, darling," he drawls.

The shame is almost as sticky as the perspiration coating me now. I want to cry. I want to come. I want to run. So many emotions you'd think one person wouldn't be able to contain them all.

"Let's get you back to the compound so you can rest," Rafferty says.

I'm suddenly so bone tired, I don't think I can walk.

The next moment, strong arms sweep me up as Ash carries me. He doesn't sling me over his shoulder the way Rafferty did. He holds me. Like I'm precious.

Can I trust it? Is this a moment of tenderness, or mind games from a boy who I fear might be as broken as I am?

Tomorrow will only bring more revelations, and I need to be stronger.

Chapter Seven
Honor

THEY DEPOSIT ME BACK in my room, and for the first time since I arrived on the island—not including the bath—I am alone.

I feel strangely detached about what has just happened, like I might be in shock. My skin feels tight from the cum that has now dried on me. Brody's cum. I remember my first thoughts upon seeing him—how he'd reminded me of the jocks who would bully me at school. My instinct had been right about that one.

I hope no one witnessed them bringing me back to the villa. They hadn't let me pull my bra back up or slip my top back on over my head, so Asher had carried me, bare-breasted and shiny with dried semen, across the beach and into the resort. I'd found myself huddled against his chest, if only to protect myself from any watching eyes. But the truth was that the only people watching were the same ones who'd set this whole thing up in the first place.

The first thing I want to do is wash.

Forgoing the bath—I need for this to be quicker, and I don't want to sit in dirty water—I turn on the shower. Its rainfall head fills the stall with thrumming water, and the glass quickly steams up. I'm grateful for that. I have no idea if there are cameras in this room, but I certainly wouldn't be surprised. I try to remember if I'd seen anything about it in the paperwork I'd signed, but it wasn't as though I'd actually read the small print. Does anyone?

Still self-conscious, I quickly strip off my clothes, leaving them in a pile on the floor, and step into the shower. The water is as hot as I can get it without it scalding me, and I exhale a sigh of pleasure as it drums onto my shoulders. I knot my hair on the top of my head to prevent it getting wet again and stand with my neck bent. The shower acts like a massager, and I allow it to work the tension from my muscles.

Despite what has come before, I have to admit that this is bliss. It's been almost two months since I left home and did my best to vanish, and things have been rough. I've found myself in plenty of precarious situations, especially after my money had run out. It's hard to say no to the offer of a couch when you've been sleeping in shop doorways for several nights on the run. Those offers mostly came from men, however, and I always knew the promise of a roof over my head and something soft to sleep on would also mean me promising something in return. I've lived in terror of being attacked and robbed, and that I've made it this far without that happening makes me think that maybe someone is looking over me. I like to think it might be my mother.

Things had ended heartbreakingly badly with her, but we'd been close once. I'd never known my dad, so, for most of my life, it had just been the two of us. I have so many cherished memories of her from when I'd been younger, of her teaching me to make pancakes in the kitchen on a Saturday morning, of her snuggled up in bed with me, reading me a bedtime story, of her allowing me to do her makeup for her, and of course me making a total mess of it. They'd been good times, carefree times, even though we'd had very little and never had money for vacations or shopping trips. But then *he* had come into her life, and everything had changed. *She* had changed.

It didn't happen overnight. For some time, things had been good. She'd been happy, and I'd been happy for her, but as months passed, and then years, I started to realize she wasn't the same person she had been.

As for him, he played things right at first. Admittedly, I was a teenager then, and I had my own shit going on, but I knew my mom needed to have her own life. And she'd seemed happy—really happy. As for me, initially he just kind of acted as though I didn't really exist, which was perfectly fine by me. Mom was occupied, so I could do what I wanted and see who I wanted, and come and go whenever I pleased, and that suited me too. Looking back, I wish I'd paid more attention. Maybe things would have had a different outcome then.

But he seemed like a respectable guy—he was a police officer, for God's sake—and Mom had been happy. When he'd suggested we all move in with him, it had made sense. His house was far bigger, and I told myself I was only going to be staying at home for a couple more years, and then I'd be out of there, anyway. It wasn't fair of me to ruin my mom's future because I liked my current bedroom.

Now I wish I had.

Tearing my thoughts from the past, I use some of the expensive soap to wash my body and face. Any trace of Brody's cum swirls down the drain. A flash of his cock jumps into my mind. It's not like I've seen a whole heap of them, but his was a particularly fine specimen. Long and thick, ridged with veins, and tipped with that smooth head. He'd smelled good, too—musky but clean. I think about what I would have done if he'd made me suck him, and I'm surprised as a tingle works its way down from my nipples to my stomach, and then lower, to tighten my core. I use the excuse of needing to wash between my legs to explore the feeling and slip my fingers between my folds and over my clit. The sensation instantly deepens ten-fold, and I draw in a tiny breath. Being so close to a gorgeous man's dick—gorgeous in looks alone, *not* personality—seems to have awoken my hormones.

I brace myself on the shower wall and rub my clit faster and harder. My tongue sweeps over my lower lip, and I start to pant. I'm taking myself back to what had happened in the cave, only now I find myself elaborating on it. Instead of just masturbating in front of me, Brody feeds me his cock, while Rafferty gets behind me and slips his hand between my thighs, finding me wet and wanting. I picture the other two looking on, their eyes hooded with lust, filled with jealousy that it's not their turn.

My movements grow faster, and every muscle in my body is taut with expectation. I'm chasing my orgasm, knowing it's right on the brink.

Then I reach it and topple over the edge, letting out a little moan as I do so.

I fall slack, breathing hard.

I slap my palm against the wall. "Shit."

Uncomfortable feelings squirm through my stomach. These men are strangers to me. I shouldn't have done that. I don't want to think about any of the men in such a way, despite what they've already done to me and what they have planned for the coming days. I need to stay focused on the money. That is my reason for doing this. God only knows how many women they've treated this way in the past, and the last thing I want is for them to think I might be getting some kind of pleasure out of it.

I remind myself that all I need to do is win each game. To not let them catch me. Then I can leave this place, untouched and a millionaire, and for the first time in what feels like forever, I'll be able to imagine a future for myself.

I turn the shower off and grab one of the fluffy white towels provided, wrapping myself in it. I step out and glance down at the pile of clothes I'd cast off. The last thing I want is to put those back on, though I have the feeling I won't be given much choice tomorrow morning. I cast my gaze around, hoping I might discover my old clothes, the ones I'd arrived here in, freshly laundered and folded somewhere for me to wear, but no such luck. Someone has taken them. In fact, I can't even see my bag—the one containing the only belongings I have.

"Fuckers."

Was that in the small print too? My phone was in that bag. Not that I exactly have anyone I can call, but I like to have it for my own reassurance. Why have they taken it? Is it because they don't want me calling the police? If only they knew how there was absolutely zero chance in hell of that ever happening. Anyway, they aren't actually doing anything illegal here, or at least I don't think they are. If I used the safeword and then they refused to let me leave, maybe that would be the time to call, but, so far, they haven't given me any indication that will happen.

In the end, I settle for a clean top that's identical to the one I'd been wearing, and another pair of ridiculously tiny panties. I don't have any other plans than to sink into the giant bed and sleep for as long as physically possible, so I don't really need anything on my lower half. Still, I find myself longing for a pair of fluffy pajamas to warm me against the chill of the air conditioning in here.

A knock comes at the door, and I stiffen. Could it be one of them?

"Come in," I call, but when the door still doesn't open, I go to answer it myself. To my surprise, there's no one there, and it takes me a moment to spot the tray that's been left on the floor.

From the parts sticking out from beneath the white cloth covering it, I can see the tray is silver. I stoop and pick it up and carry it back into the room with me. I say room, but this place is bigger than any apartment I've ever stayed in. I carry the tray over to the small dining table, set it down, and whip off the cloth.

"Oh, my God."

My mouth waters. I've been treated to a seafood platter on ice—lobster, crab, shrimp, oysters. Nestled among the seafood is a small dish of black caviar, wedges of bright yellow lemon, and buttered triangles of thinly sliced whole wheat bread. The oysters have already been dressed with what appears to be white vinegar and shallots. I'm still not sure I'm brave enough to try one, however. On a separate plate is a slice of dark chocolate pie together with whipped cream and ripe strawberries.

This is my reward, I realize. My reward for playing their game, showing them my tits, and taking a face-full of cum. That and two hundred thousand dollars, or, if I make it to the end, a million.

Right now, I'm highly doubting my ability to make it to the end. I'm not sure I'll even make it through tomorrow. What happened today shook me, and they said it was only a taster. I don't even want to think about what else they might have planned for me. One thing I am sure of, whatever innocence I've come to this island with isn't going to last for long.

I've been so focused on sleep that I haven't given my hunger much thought, but now I have a feast laid out in front of me, I realize how famished I am. Working backward, I start with the chocolate pie, whipped cream, and strawberries. It's rich and not too sweet, and I finish it within the space of two minutes. I drink some water and then start in on the shellfish. It's fresh and delicious, and I work my way through it, squeezing lemon onto the lobster and shrimp, and scooping caviar onto the triangles of bread. I give the oysters a sniff but decide to give them a miss.

With my stomach full, I can now barely keep my eyes open. I visit the bathroom to quickly wash my hands and face, and brush my teeth, and then I crawl into bed.

The bed is huge, the mattress soft, the bedding pure white with a satin feel. I sink into it and groan with pleasure.

Only seconds pass before oblivion claims me.

Chapter Eight
Honor

"YOU'RE GOING TO BE late!"

A shrill voice launches me from sleep, and I jerk upright, blinking my eyes open.

Felicity is standing next to my bed, her hands on her hips. Her lips are pinched in disapproval.

It takes my brain a moment to catch up to my body, and I try to remember where I am and why I'm here.

The island.

The men...Oh, God, the men.

Despite everything, I discover I've slept like the dead. How many hours have I been out? Bright sunlight filters through the drapes, but I've no idea what time it is. There are no clocks in the room, and now my phone has been taken away, I don't have any way of telling the time. Is this another way of disorienting me?

"What am I late for?" I manage to murmur, my voice thick with sleep.

"The first game," she says. "Up, up, up!"

I half expect her to whip away the bedcovers, but she doesn't. With a sigh, I throw them back and climb out of bed.

"Do I have time to use the bathroom?"

She gives me a glare of exasperation. "Of course. You couldn't possibly think I'd allow you to start the game looking like that." She flaps a hand in my general direction.

I guess that means I'm not looking my best.

On the way to the bathroom, I note that the leftover tray is no longer in the room. Did Felicity remove it? Or has someone else come into the room while I was sleeping? The thought unnerves me. It was bad enough waking up to Felicity standing over me, without thinking about a stranger moving around the room while I was so deeply asleep.

I'm grateful to close the bathroom door behind me, shutting off the sight of Felicity's irritated face. I'm not quite sure what it is I've done to upset her so much. I imagine her reaction when she finds out about the mix-up. I've fed myself the story that this will be easy and I just have to win each game to make it through to the end with my innocence intact, but there is one major thing that will screw everything up. If they find out I'm really supposed to just be a maid here, all bets are off. I might have signed a contract, but will they still honor the two hundred thousand dollars if they discover who I really am? I might be putting myself through all of this, only to come out of it with even less than if I'd owned up to the mistake. At least if I'd been honest, I'd still have a job and a roof over my head. I'd be in a place where my stepfather would struggle to find me.

The magnitude of what I'm taking on hits me, and my stomach churns, my breath growing short. I pause with my hands on the edge of the sink, my head lowered as I try to hold on to my grip of the world. My palms are cold and clammy against the porcelain, and an iron band has wrapped itself around my chest, constricting my lungs.

Too much, too much, too much.

But I've been through a lot in these past few months—no, I correct myself, not just months. It's been *years*—ever since he wormed his way into our lives. I'd thought, when he'd asked us to come and live with him, that he wouldn't want some teenage girl hanging around, but I'd been wrong. But as I grew older, I started to wonder if having a teenager living with him had all been part of the plan. At first, I thought the accidental walk-ins into the bathroom were just that—accidental. He'd said the lock had been broken for ages and made promises to fix it. When he never did, despite me repeatedly asking, I'd ended up doing it myself. He'd thrown a fit about it, saying he'd been planning on doing it that coming weekend and that I shouldn't be screwing around with things on his property. It hadn't just been that, either. I'd often discover pieces of my underwear going missing from the laundry, but when I questioned where they'd gone, he'd denied knowing anything. By this point, he'd also started chipping away at my mother, so when I mentioned my concerns to her, she took his side. Maybe I should have left then and there, but I had no money of my own, and besides, I didn't want to leave my mom. I could see what he was doing to her, and though I wished she'd be stronger and walk away, I loved her and didn't want to abandon her to him.

I jump at a loud bang at the bathroom door.

"What are you doing in there?"

I realize I've just been standing at the sink, lost in a swirling whirlwind of memories and fears. I haven't even managed to wash my face yet.

"Won't be long," I manage to call back.

My voice is shaky, and I exhale a long breath, trying to keep myself together. I've been through worse, I remind myself.

I'm strong. I can do this.

I use the toilet and then run the faucet to wash my hands and splash water on my face. Then I use the toothbrush and toothpaste provided. I glimpse myself in the mirror. My skin is even paler than normal—I definitely don't have the Californian tan—but otherwise I appear well-rested. The dark circles that have been prominent beneath my eyes for so long have vanished thanks to the good sleep on a comfortable bed, and my skin is clear.

Maybe the semen facial I got the day before did it some good.

I give my reflection a wry smile and then go back into the bedroom. Felicity has laid a new outfit on the bed, ready for me. It's identical to the one I'd been wearing yesterday.

I remember something. "Where are all my belongings?" I ask her. "My bag and old clothes, and my phone."

She sniffs. "You won't be needing them until it's time for you to leave."

"Maybe I won't need them, but they're mine, and I want them."

"You already agreed to it. You belong to the gentlemen now, and that includes your possessions. They get to dress you, to tell you when and what to eat, and when to sleep. You're not your own person any longer."

I grit my teeth. "Right."

With little other choice, I get dressed.

"You know I can do this in private," I say to Felicity. "I'm twenty-one years old. I've been dressing myself for quite some time now."

"It's my job to make sure you do everything right. If you prevent me from doing my job, and you screw up, it'll be my head it lands on."

I don't know how I can possibly screw up getting dressed, but I can tell by her wide-legged stance and folded arms that she's not budging.

When I'm done, she motions at me. "Hair," she barks.

I let out a sigh and put my back to her as she produces a hairbrush and hair-tie seemingly out of nowhere. Normally, I find it relaxing to have my hair played with, but Felicity scrapes at my scalp and yanks my hair back so hard it hurts. I know there's no point in protesting, so I grit my teeth and let her get on with pulling my hair back into a high ponytail. I assume the hairstyle will make it easier for the men to grab me during a chase.

The thought sends a fresh cascade of nerves through me. I can hardly believe I'm going through with this.

One million dollars. Eyes on the prize.

At some point, they're going to figure out that I'm lying. Either the girl who was supposed to be playing this game will show up, apologizing for being late, but saying she's ready to start, or they'll wonder why the new maid hasn't shown up for her job. A thought occurs to me, and I hold back a curse. The phone number I gave them as a contact is the same one that is in the bag they've now taken and stored away somewhere. When the maid—i.e. me—doesn't show up in two days, they're bound to try the phone number I gave them to find out what's happened to me. What if the bag is stashed in an office somewhere and, when they call the phone, the bag starts ringing? I'll be busted then, for sure.

If I'm going to make it to the end of this, I have to get hold of my phone.

Felicity releases me, and I turn to face her. "I really could use getting my bag back, if only for a few minutes. There's someone I need to message to tell them I'm safe."

She gestures to the landline phone sitting on a desk. "You can make a call from here."

I don't want to make a call. I want to get my hands on the phone so I can at least switch it off. That way, if they try to call, it'll just go through to a generic voicemail. But I do find myself glancing back at the phone. Could I risk calling Ruth from here? I wonder if the calls are traceable. While I trust my best friend with my life, I would never forgive myself if I put her in any kind of danger. If my stepfather thought she knew something, he'd go to any lengths to get that information from her. I long to hear a friendly voice with all my heart, but I just can't risk it.

Felicity appraises me once more. "Okay, you'll do. Let's go."

"What happens now?" I ask, speaking to her back as she exits the bedroom and heads down the corridor.

A cleaner is busy dusting the tables dotted along one side of the space, but she's wearing a black pinafore and a white apron—nothing like my outfit. I try to catch her eye and smile, but she doesn't even glance up.

Felicity speaks over her shoulder. "You'll be given your instructions for the day."

I hurry to catch up, so we're walking side by side. "By whom?"

She shoots me a quizzical look. "Who do you think?"

It dawns on me that I'm about to be back in the presence of the four men. My insides quiver. How will I be able to look them in the eye after yesterday? They've seen me half naked with cum all over my face. I'm mortified just thinking about it. But then there's the possibility I have far worse to come.

We make our way back through the building and up to the office I'd met them in the previous day. Felicity knocks and then pushes the door open, and nods for me to enter.

On shaking legs, I do.

The men are all here. Rafferty stands in the middle of the room, his dark hair swept back from his face. He's dressed in what appears to be his customary suit, only this one is in navy, the color setting off the oceanic blue of his eyes. He stands straight, broad shoulders back, his chin lifted. In the short amount of time I've spent in their presence, I've already learned Rafferty seems to be the one in charge. He exudes authority.

My gaze is drawn to Brody, who's leaning against a wall and is more casually dressed in light blue jeans and a tight gray t-shirt that's stretched across the breadth of his chest and shoulders and hugs every muscle. My eyes flick down to the front of his jeans, making sure he's all covered up today. He catches me looking and a slow smile forms in the corners of his lips. Bastard.

"Honor," Rafferty says, cocking his head in my direction. "We trust you're well rested."

"Yes," I manage to squeak. "I slept well."

"Good. You'll need to be feeling strong for today."

"For the first game?" I confirm.

"For the first *hunt*," Wilder growls from where he's sitting on a black leather swivel chair that looks as though it must have been made to fit his size.

Hunt. I shiver at the word.

Wilder's black ribbed tank top and black jeans and boots mean he almost blends in with his seat. I find my gaze roaming over the swell of his biceps and the myriad of tattoos that cover his skin. One in particular catches my attention—a triangle with an eye in the middle. I feel like I've seen it somewhere before. I muse on it for a moment and then remember. Of course, it was on the side of the plane that brought me over from the mainland. I wonder what it means.

Brody covers his crotch with his hand and gives himself a squeeze. "You know we're going to do everything in our power to catch you. I can't wait to get a taste of you."

Asher looks up from his phone, and his tongue sneaks across his full lower lip. "I hope we get more than a taste."

I can't quite figure Asher out—not that I've really figured any of them out. I remember the way he carried me back to the resort, with me huddled against his chest to try to hide my semi-nudity. Asher is a slighter build than the others and not as tall, though still far taller than I am. At first glance, it would be easy to dismiss him as being the more reserved, younger, weaker one with his glasses and button-up shirt, but there had been no mistaking the strength in his muscles as he'd carried me. There's something about his eyes as well, their warm brown tones filled with gentleness one minute, and flashing to hard steel the next. I have to wonder which version is the real Asher.

BLURRED LIMITS

All four of them stare at me with hunger. I've never known such intensity before. It's like being trapped in a room with four lions, who all haven't eaten for some time.

"Just like yesterday," Rafferty says, "we'll give you a head start. Since you'll be covering a much bigger distance than yesterday, we'll give you an hour. Let me just warn you, the terrain isn't easy going, so be careful. The last thing any of us wants is for you to get injured."

What would they do if I did get hurt and was unable to run? Would they still consider that they'd caught me and do whatever they wanted to me? Perhaps I'd understand if it was a twisted ankle, but what if I was more seriously hurt? What if I fractured my skull or knocked myself unconscious? Would they get me some help, or would they just use and abuse me however they wanted? Just how sick are these men? I'm genuinely too frightened to ask. I decide I just have to make sure I don't injure myself.

I'm starting to create a list of rules. Don't get caught. Don't get hurt.

What's going to be next?

Wilder stands from his chair and snatches up a backpack from the floor beside him. He approaches to hand it to me, and I find myself rearing back. I'm guessing he's about two hundred and fifty pounds of muscle. That would be intimidating enough, but there are also the tattoos that cover every part of his skin except for his face. I'm glad his face isn't marked, because it really is an extraordinarily handsome one. His eyes are an unusual shade of green, like forest leaves when the sun shines through them—and they're framed by a fringe of thick brown lashes. His lower lip is fuller than his top lip and has a crease in the center that makes me think about what it would be like to suck it.

"Here," he says, shoving the bag at me and tearing me from my thoughts. "You'll need this."

I nod and glance inside. Like yesterday, it's supplies for survival—some food, water, a baseball cap to keep the sun off my face. I'm relieved to spot some sunscreen as well. With my pale skin, I burn if I so much as stand near a bright lightbulb.

"Thanks," I mutter.

"Here's the map." Rafferty hands it to me.

I unfold it and cast my gaze across the paper. Sure enough, there's a red cross on it. It looks like it's across the other side of the island. Immediately, I start to strategize. Will it be better to go through the middle of the island, or head down to the beach and work my way around the coast? Both options have pitfalls. The coast sounds like a more pleasant option—since there's sand and ocean to dip my feet into when I get too hot—but from what I can work out, there's also a section that turns to cliff and rock, and that could be perilous. I could try to swim around it, but that holds its dangers, too. I could end up being swept against the cliff face, or I might end up being stung by jellyfish or worse.

Going through the middle of the island also looks difficult. On the other side of the resort—the part that's built into the rock of the island—the landmass rises to jagged, rocky peaks. I'm no mountain climber, and Rafferty's warning about not getting injured echoes in my ears. But going that way would mean I'd be covering a shorter distance. A shorter distance could mean a shorter hunt, and I'd get to the item quicker.

"What are you waiting for?" Wilder grunts.

I glance up from the map, my cheeks flushing with heat. I've been dismissed.

I spin on my toes and hurry from the office, relieved to be free of them, at least for the time being. I realize I only have minutes to make my decision about which direction I should take. If I go the wrong way, I'll be forced to double back on myself, and then there will be a good chance of bumping right into them on the way back. There's something else I need to consider—which way will they think I'll go? They might assume I'll take the coastal route and come after me that way, and if I'm actually heading through the middle of the island, there'll be no chance of them catching me, unless they happen to reach the X first, which is always a possibility. Or maybe they'll split up, and two will take the coastal route and the other two will hike through the island.

There's also a good chance they'll cheat and use whatever cameras are on the island to track my progress. Then they'll know exactly which route I've taken and how far along I've managed to get.

I wonder what will happen the next time I meet these four. Will I be celebrating my win, or will I be pinned down and terrified?

Despite myself, a tingle wakens within me, and my core throbs. I remember how they'd gotten me to admit my fantasy in the cave. How was it possible that they knew about that? Was it intuition? Then it dawns on me that they must have had some contact with whoever the woman is I'm currently pretending to be. They would have discussed exactly what they liked and what they wanted to get out of this.

To my surprise, a flash of jealousy, jagged and sharp, rips through me. I don't like the idea of them talking to another woman like that. I give myself a mental slap. Stupid of me. There must have been plenty of women who'd come before me, and many more who'd come after.

Chapter Nine
Brody

I LAUGH AS HONOR STUMBLES. She's only been out there five minutes, and already she's tripping on things and taking wrong turns. She consults the map hastily, crumples it up, and shoves it in her bag, then she's moving again.

"That girl really does appear desperate not to get caught," Asher observes. "It makes me want to catch her all the more. Wonder if it's really a kink with her, or she's just all about the money."

I think it's a kink. That's my instinct. One can never tell, however. We talk to them a lot online before they arrive here, but how the fuck do we know if they're telling the truth? We all cover our identities on the dark net, and make sure not to show our whole faces during any exchanges. We even use a voice changing app so there's no chance of someone accidentally recognizing one of our voices. It does leave us open to the possibility of being catfished, however, no money changes hands until they leave the island, and we've all got what we want by then.

This one does intrigue me. She also worries me. Something's off. I spent a lot of time having to be able to quickly analyze people while in the military, and my sense of her is someone who doesn't know what the fuck she's doing. More than that, I saw how hot she was for it all yesterday, and I think that's what scares her the most. Whether it all started purely for the money or not, she's in over her head now because she's actually into the chase, the hunt, the humiliation.

Poor bitch.

She'll earn every penny of that two hundred K, in that case. No way will she get the million. None of them ever do.

"Asher and I will take the coast," Rafferty states. "You and Wilder take the direct path across to the rendezvous point."

He's always acting like the big fucking boss of us all. Normally, it doesn't bother me, but today, I'm in a shitty mood. I don't know why, but I didn't sleep well last night. Something maybe to do with the morsel on the screen running from us.

I wanted more than the little bit of fun we had yesterday, and even though I'd already come, I took care of myself in the shower, imagining things going much farther.

There's something about the girl that gets to me. She's scared. Unsure. Tiny, as well. But on the other hand, there's this air about her, almost an aloofness. No, it's not that, I realize. It's an otherworldliness, as if she somehow exists on another plane. It concerns me as well. There's a part of me that worries this girl will be our downfall. She could be our Pandora, ready to open her box in order to escape us.

I glance at my watch. She's making good progress, but not quite as fast as yesterday. That's the thing; it wears them down. They get stressed and don't sleep too well. They have to do this over and over again, day after day. Although we do, too, for us there's not the adrenaline and stress the same way there is for our prey. It's hard to run from your hunters all day, and then get up and do the same thing all over again. It grinds you down. I know.

The thoughts come thick and fast, and my hands ball into fists. Fuck. It's been a while since I had a momentary flashback so strong, and it's not even associated with anything. Normally, it's a noise, or a smell.

Burning meat. That one always nicely takes me back. You won't find me manning the grill anytime soon. I hate the Fourth of July because fireworks have me breaking out in a cold sweat. Things aren't as bad for me now as they were when I first came home. I remember one day walking through a park, and a group of teenagers had one of those portable barbecues. The scent of the beef they were searing hit me so hard. I'd started shaking, and to make matters worse, I was on a date.

The stench of flesh burning hit my nose, and I'd bent double, grabbing hold of a nearby tree to stop myself falling to my knees. I tried to breathe through my mouth and calm my roiling stomach, but it didn't work. Two seconds later, I'd thrown up everywhere. The images flickering across my closed eyelids, as I'd wiped my mouth and attempted to straighten, took me to a different place and time.

I had no longer stood in a park full of greenery, with children playing around me, but instead found myself in a dusty landscape, my nostrils clogged with fine sand as I drove the Jeep. The next moment, we were airborne, and my best friend, sitting behind me, was thrown out of the vehicle. I'd braked, jumped out, and run over to him, but as I got near, he turned onto his front and began, for some reason, to pull himself forward across the ground.

From there on, the flashbacks always go into horrifying slow motion. I opened my mouth to scream at him, but the wave from the blast hit me, sending me flying. I'd been blown backward off my feet, and for a moment lay in the sand, dazed.

Then the smell hit. Burning, searing flesh.

It coated me inside and out, and I knew as long as I lived that I would never get it out of my nose.

Every time I smell that particular scent, my body reacts in the same way.

I reach for the ID tags I still wear beneath my shirt and hold them in my fist like they're a talisman. Damn Honor for making me feel this way when there aren't barbecues or fireworks for tens of miles.

I'll make her pay. I might up things a notch the next time I get to play with her.

As we wait, I take my phone out and peruse the headlines. Nothing but grief, and violence, and unhappiness. The way my life used to be, before I found my brothers in this room. Four men who share certain tastes. But it goes beyond that. Our bond reaches into our past, to places none of us visit anymore, unless we really must.

One of these days, we will have to, if we wish to find the fucker who screwed us all up in the first place.

I shake the thoughts off. Christ, I'm a whiny bitch today. I don't even want to be in my own head, I'm that much of a downer. I glance at the markets, and then read a ridiculous story on the news app about a woman who sells her breath in a jar to sad men who have nothing else to spend their money on. They ought to make sure they get something worthwhile, the way we do every year when we hold the hunt.

"It's time we set off after baby girl," Asher says with a quick glance at his watch.

His words pull me out of my reverie, and I bring myself back to the reality of the room and the space I'm in. I let my feet feel the floor, and my eyes take in certain objects in the room. The sound of birds outside is soothing to my ears, and for a few short but happy moments, I drink it all in.

Mindfulness. Being present. All great antidotes to stress, panic, and anxiety.

It's supposed to help with PTSD, so I try it most days. Sometimes I think it does make a difference, but mostly I don't.

"See you at the rendezvous," I say, slapping Asher on the back as Wilder and I head for the door.

We are cutting straight across the island and will hopefully reach her before the others do. I'd quite like a chance to play the start of this game with Wilder and without Rafferty there. He's an overbearing dick sometimes.

As we head out of the door of the compound and into the bright light of mid-morning, I realize it is considerably hotter than the average, and I'm grateful for the baseball cap that I wear more often than not. This is more like a hot day in Greece than your average mid-seventies Fahrenheit we usually get off this part of the California coast.

Wilder bends and touches the ground where her feet have left indents in the soil along the edge of the vegetation which surrounds the compound. Wilder doesn't need to physically track her. We have cameras to tell us where she is at any given time we ask. However, he prefers it this way. He likes the thrill of the chase. A real chase, the old-fashioned way.

Still, it pays to know the location of the prey, in case they panic and try to do something epically stupid like leave on one of the boats and forfeit all the cash. That was Asher and his damned weird shit. The woman got so freaked out about it she'd tried to run from us. Rafferty paid her an extra fifty grand, as we were worried about that one talking.

What will Honor's breaking point be?

We follow in her footsteps as Wilder enjoys his old-school tracking, and I try to figure her out. It's not long before thinking deserts me as we maintain a fast jog, carrying supplies, across a sweltering island.

The track isn't easygoing. We hike higher through the rocky center of the island, occasionally forced to slow down and literally climb up boulders and rocky outcrops that rise from the earth. With our longer legs and good upper-body strength, this isn't a problem for me or Wilder, but tiny Honor will have found it more of a challenge. We're betting on her finding this harder than we do. It's the reason we're confident we'll catch up with her.

I pause on the top of one of the boulders, taking in the view of the island from this position. Leafy fronds of palm trees sway in the breeze, and in the distance is the blue of the ocean. I scan the terrain, trying to spot any movement that might indicate our prey's location, but nothing gives her away.

"You snoozing over there?" Wilder calls over his shoulder.

He's gotten ahead of me, and I don't like trailing behind. If Wilder catches her first, he'll be the one who gets the first go at her, and if what she claims about her being a virgin is true, she'll never be able to handle his monster cock as her first time. I smirk internally as I picture her face when she sees it, piercings and all.

I break back into a jog and catch up to Wilder. He pulls his long hair into a ponytail, exposing his undercut, and then we keep going.

By the time I'm sure we're gaining on her, I've found myself enjoying the run. This is nothing to me. I used to have to move for many miles carrying a heavy load when in the military, but it's hot today, and there's little breeze.

Wilder stops me by putting his arm out, and I pause to let him take a drink.

"You should hydrate," he says.

"Every stop is letting her get farther ahead."

"She won't outrun us."

I glance down at the map and check how close we are to the prize she's chasing. I'm glad we got the harder but more direct overland route to the spot, as we will likely get there before Rafferty and Asher taking the coastal route.

"She's fit, though, no? Faster than any other girl we've had here."

I nod and decide I will take a drink of my own water. My throat is dry. I take it out of the rucksack and swallow it down gratefully. Then I replace the cap, stash it, and haul the pack back onto my back. One of us draws the short straw each hunt of carrying the big pack, and this time it's me. "She is. Can read a map too, unlike some of the idiots who come here."

Wilder snorts.

A couple of months back, we had five tech execs hire us to do our usual job, which is a simulated evade and capture weekend for the bored super rich, who get to pretend they're being chased by enemy forces for real. If they get caught, we interrogate them, and if they manage to last the entire interrogation without using the safeword, they get their place on the weekend for free. So far, only three out of a few hundred have not paid.

This one group couldn't even read a map. These were super intelligent guys. Serious nerds, like Asher, who'd made a fortune, but they fucked up left, right, and center and we caught them far too early in the game. We let them go again because otherwise our whole weekend would have been spent pretend torturing those idiots.

The interrogations can be intense. That's where I come in. I use the skills I was taught in the special forces, and I've trained the other three in them, too. We don't go so far as waterboarding, but we use sensory deprivation, hitting them with objects in a controlled way so they won't harm but will hurt and bruise. Loud music. Horrible sounds like babies screaming. I'm always amazed how many people break within the first hour of having their hands tied behind their backs, feet pushed apart by a spreader bar, eyes covered, head covered, and then heavy metal blasted through earphones, or sirens, or a baby crying. Some only last five or ten minutes. I wonder how long Honor would last bound and gagged, sitting in the dark.

"Those idiots all tapped out super early, too." Wilder roll his eyes.

I don't answer, just nod.

He scowls at me. "What gives? You're in a weird mood today."

I exam him for a long moment, then decide to tell him at least a little of my worries. Wilder is the one out of the three I get on with the best, maybe because I know, like me, he could be dropped almost anywhere on this Earth and survive. I respect that in a person.

"I think there's something off about her. Nothing I can put my finger on. She's just...I don't know, something doesn't seem right."

"Maybe she's got here and realized she's in over her head. Wouldn't be the first time."

I shrug. "Yeah, maybe."

Wilder studies me now.

"Is that why you've been hesitant?" he says. "I was getting worried. Thinking you were going soft on us."

I laugh. "Nah, that's your job."

He punches me, hard, on the arm. "Come on, fucker, let's get moving again."

Not long after we take off at a jog, Wilder pauses and bends down. Fresh footprints. "She's not been long past here."

We cover ground swiftly now, knowing she's in our sights. She's close to the final goal as well, though, so I know we need to act fast.

The blood rushes in my veins. I love this. The chase. The final moments when we're closing in.

Wilder does, too. He might like to come across all Zen, but he's as fucked up as the rest of us, otherwise he wouldn't be here.

To my right, I spot movement. A dash of silky dark hair in the sun, like a raven's wing, flashing for a moment before she sees us and pivots. I grin and don't even say a word to Wilder. I simply take off at full speed right after her.

I crash through the thick undergrowth as a shortcut to reach her. I plow into her, grabbing her in my arms, and she lets out a yell of shock.

Her words are cut short by us hitting the ground. My baseball cap flies off. Then I roll, ensuring she's not hurt. My arms are full of squirming woman, and I love it. I kiss her neck just for shits and giggles.

"Ugh, get off me." She struggles harder, and I can't tell if this is playacting or for real.

I laugh and turn her to face me, so her baby blues are looking right at me.

"Hey, there, Pandora." I grin. "Time for some fun."

Piercing pain hits me right between the legs.

Holy fuck.

For a moment, the world fuzzes out, and I need to take two or three deep breaths in order not to throw up.

Automatically, I open my arms and grab my junk, and she's back on her feet. Honor takes off, flying through the bushes, not even looking back to see if she's unmanned me for life.

That sneaky little bitch. She kicked me in the nuts. I guess she really was struggling for real.

"Christ," I spit out as I curl up. She got me good and hard.

"You okay there, buddy?" Wilder's dry tone has me wanting to punch him. Luckily for him, I still can't move.

"She kicked me in the fucking balls." I finally push myself to my knees, and then a standing position, teeth gritted against the pain. I scoop down and grab my hat and yank it down hard over my head again.

He cracks up laughing. "You're white as a sheet, man. She got you good."

"Where the fuck were you?" I rasp.

"You caught me by surprise. You should have said you'd spotted her."

I realize I hadn't said a word. Was that because I'd wanted her all to myself? My selfish choice had backfired, though. If Wilder had been with me, he could have caught her again, and I might have even spared myself the foot to the balls.

I suck air in over my teeth. "I'm going to have fun with her when I catch her."

I'm going to make that little minx pay for this. She has no idea how depraved I can get, but she might be about to find out.

"Which way did she go?" I ask Wilder.

"Toward the beach. You go toward the headland, and I'll take the bluff."

Perfect. She can't get away if she traps herself on the beach. Dead ends both sides with one of us each either end.

"Let's go," I shout at Wilder as I take off in that direction, my nuts still killing me.

The palm trees and bushes grow more sparce, and the shush of waves breaking on shore meets my ears. I break through the trees and stop for a moment, looking down the white sands. At first, I think she's not here, then I spy her. She's low, in the grasses that border the tops of the dunes on the far section of the long stretch.

Gotcha.

I don't bother to hide my presence, knowing she can't outrun me. I set off toward her at full speed.

Not turning around, she must hear me coming, because she bolts. She glances behind to look at me, her long ponytail swinging. I'm going to wrap that hair around her damn throat and lead her around by it after what she did.

I reach her, and for the second time that day, I take her down to the ground. This time, though, I don't bother to cushion the impact for her. The sand is soft and deep here on the dunes, and she won't come to any harm.

I want her to feel my full weight as I pin her to the ground.

She makes a small *oomph* sound as we hit, and then I'm trapping her in place. I find her wrists and hold them above her head as I stare down at her.

"Gotcha, Pan," I say.

Expecting fear, I'm surprised to see a smile crawl across her pretty features. What the hell?

Then I realize she's holding something in one of the hands I have pinned down.

No way. No, fucking way. She got the prize.

Honor is holding the long, pointed prize wrapped in shiny red paper.

Disappointment hits me hard. No games today. She won.

Wilder catches up to us, and I turn to him in time to see him realize she's holding the prize.

She laughs. "You better let me up, *sir*."

The *sir* has an edge of sarcasm to it that I want to choke out of her.

"She found the prize?" a voice says from a distance.

I glance to my right to see Asher and Rafferty approach us from around the bluff where the cliff at the edge of the beach meets the sea. There's a way across, but if you don't know the rocks there, it can be treacherous, and it looks, to all intents and purposes, as if you can't pass.

Asher is staring at Honor's hand in narrow-eyed focus.

"I did," she states, all proud of herself. "So, I get to go back and pamper myself and rest."

"You do," I say as I get off her. I hold my hand out to her and help her up. "Well done."

"Thank you." She seems blindsided by my attitude.

Did she expect me to keep the game going? No, she won this round fair and square, so for a short while, there's a truce.

For now.

"Long walk back. We can take the boat if you'd prefer?" Rafferty asks her.

She glances at us all, unsure.

So she should be. We're going to be all nice and polite with her now, until the games begin again tomorrow, and we aren't doing it because we're deep-down nice guys. No, we have ulterior motives.

One, throw her off her guard some.

Two, we hope if she relaxes enough now, she'll use the very special prize she's holding when she gets back to her room.

Chapter Ten
Honor

"THERE'S A BOAT HERE?" I ask Rafferty, looking around, my hands on my hips.

I'm out of breath from the run, and hot and sticky. The ocean looks tempting right now, and a part of me wants to just dive right in.

"Yep, a dinghy, over there." He points to the reeds farther along the bay, and I squint. As I look, I see it. A small, black rubber craft hidden in the long grasses and weeds.

"Oh, okay." My legs are sore, and I'm tired out now the adrenaline has crashed.

"You look like you need the boat option," Wilder says. "Adrenaline crash, gets you every time."

It's like he read my mind.

"It's normal," he carries on. "You've been running. And then you find the prize, so you know the games are off for today. I bet you'll be asleep within an hour of getting home."

I nod, and as if my body is following his words, I yawn.

"Come on, let's get you back," Brody says. "Well done."

I flush with fresh heat as I remember what I did to him. "Are your...erm...you know...are you okay?"

He laughs. "Are you asking me if I need surgery to re-attach my balls? No, I don't, but damn, it hurt."

"Sorry." I really *am* sorry I hurt him, too. I don't like to hurt anyone, but I had to get away.

I had realized when I glanced at the map about two minutes before Brody collided into me that I was close to the end of this hunt, and the rendezvous point where the prize was hidden. The moment he took me down, I was determined to fight with all I had. No way could I be so close to winning but not make it.

The map for today's game showed me clearly where the prize would be, and it was there, buried under a few inches of sand. The red paper became visible as I scrabbled at the sand beneath the large Mexican bush sage plant, which was marked on the map as the place to look.

As the men drag the boat from the dunes out onto the water, I stroke the shiny paper. I love getting presents. Always have. I didn't get many growing up, mostly because before *him*, money was tight, and after *him*, things went to shit.

"Don't open it yet," Asher states. "That's for opening this evening, while you relax. That's an order, okay?"

I nod at him. "Yes, of course."

Once they have the dinghy on the water, Rafferty takes my hand and helps me in. It's a bit of a squeeze, and I find myself squished next to Brody, which isn't ideal, given that, not that long ago, I kicked him between the legs.

I remember him calling me something as he took me down. "What did you call me?" I ask him. "Pan?"

He arches an eyebrow. "Short for Pandora."

"Pandora? Why Pandora?"

BLURRED LIMITS 115

"Because I think you might be our downfall."

"Oh."

I have no idea how to respond to that.

The conversation is polite, almost pleasantly bland, as if we're on a day trip together, and not one woman, amongst four big men who intend to hunt her down day after day for sport.

"Do you like your room?" Rafferty asks as Wilder steers us using the engine attached to the rudder.

"It's gorgeous." It is, so why lie and pretend I don't like it?

"What will you do with your time off?" Asher asks.

I think for a moment. "Am I allowed to use the pool?"

Asher and Rafferty exchange a glance.

"You can," Rafferty says. "You don't have a swimsuit."

"I can swim in my underwear." I shrug.

"Nope. You can't. The rule we have is you can use the pool, but naked." Rafferty gives me a friendly smile as if he's just told me they ask you to take your shoes off after entering the hallway.

"Are you serious?"

"Deadly," Asher says. "You want to swim, you can, but naked."

"Do *you* have to swim naked, or is it just the little lady?" I can't keep back the bite of my response.

Damn, I need to stop being so bitchy. At this rate they'll want me gone and probably pay me the lower amount just to leave.

"No, we swim naked, too." Wilder turns and flashes me a grin.

Is he lying or being truthful? I gaze out at the water and pretend I don't really care. I'd love to swim and catch some sun.

"If it makes you feel better, we've all got a conference call this afternoon," Brody whispers in my ear. "So, if you want to swim, say around three, we won't be there to watch you."

"As if I can trust you."

"One thing to know about me," he says, deadly serious. "I don't lie. Ever. Can't fucking stand liars. We have a conference call. You'll be safe to swim. And if you've never been naked in the water like that, it's a great feeling. You can lie on a lounger afterward and enjoy the sun on your skin, too. It's freeing."

"Won't the staff see me if someone comes out there?" I ask.

"No one does while it is in use. A rule we put in place, so we don't go around flashing our junk to the staff. Can you imagine Felicity getting an eyeful of it?" He gives a deep chuckle.

I can't help but smile at the thought of Ms. Felicity-Stick-Up-Her-Ass coming face-to-face with any of these lot naked. She'd probably have a heart attack.

"So, you really do swim naked?"

"Like to keep the tan all over," he replies.

His words put images into my mind I didn't need. Sensual images of the four very different men all laid around the pool without any clothes on topping up their tans.

"Oh, and just so you know, the first time I get to properly play with you, you're going to pay for what you did to my poor balls."

I swallow hard and look back out to the sea.

Chapter Eleven
Honor

AFTER A GORGEOUS COUPLE of hours around the pool, where I read, sunbathed, and swam, all naked, I return to my room wrapped in a towel, averting my gaze when I pass a couple of members of smartly dressed staff walking by. Brody was correct. It was freeing to be naked in the sun and then to do lazy laps in the pool and feel the water caress me all over. It had taken a little while for me to relax fully—a part of me certain one of the staff would catch me, or that it was a trick, and the men would show up to take advantage. But by the time half an hour had passed and there had been no sign of anyone, I'd shucked off my towel and slipped into the cool water. I'd emerged, refreshed, and it had seemed a shame to cover myself back up with the towel instead of allowing the sun to dry me.

Now, I'm turned on. Whether from the sun on my skin, or the water caressing me, or the hunt earlier today, I don't know, but the ache between my legs is growing insistent. Maybe it would have been better to let them win?

I glance at the prize on the table in the entrance to the room and trail my finger over it. What is it?

Asher said I'm forbidden from opening it until this evening.

I yawn and decide I'll have a nap and then maybe a soak in the bath, as the previous day I eschewed it in favor of the shower after Brody came all over me.

The disgusting pig.

As angry and ashamed as I feel every time I think about it, I also get a twinge at my core. A fierce ache that makes me wish he'd do it to me again, only this time make me suck him in to my mouth and take him all the way down my throat.

I'm on edge, all worked up and in need of relief, but too scared to let them catch me to get it. I'm beginning to guess exactly what is going on here. Their whole thing is chasing the woman down, then making her give in to them. I'm guessing that's the thing of the women who come here, too.

They think I'm someone else. Someone who likes being chased, tackled to the ground, and then taken by four big men.

I'm not who they think I am…I'm nothing but the maid, but in truth, I *am* a woman who has had that particular fantasy more than once.

Okay, not the whole four men on an island part, but I've definitely fantasized about being forced to do things. It's a thing of mine. A secret, dark desire, and one which I've always hidden away, even from myself at times.

It's hard to admit, particularly when you've been through what I have. Who in their right mind still has coercion fantasies after their stepfather tried that very thing?

A fucked-up person, that's who.

I sigh and decide I need a rest. I head into the bedroom, drop the towel, and crawl between the sheets. The moment my head hits the pillow, my eyes drift closed.

When I awake, it's dark outside. Shit, how long did I sleep?

I don't want to waste the whole evening snoozing, so I get up and pad into the living area, where I pause when I see the food and wine set out on the table. God, whoever does all this this is like a ninja. So quiet. It's creepy I didn't even know someone was in here again.

I pour a glass of wine and sip. It's the same sweet and heady white wine I shared with Felicity the other day. Taking the glass with me, I head into the bathroom and run myself a bath, pouring in some of the fragranced oil Felicity procured for me to go with the other lotions and potions I have. All in that signature scent...what was it called? Angel and Demon.

I slide into the water and sigh. The temperature is perfect, and the scent wraps around me beautifully. It's a sublime fragrance. Warm in my watery slice of heaven, I let my hands run over my skin, reveling in how silky my touch is on my own body with the oil gliding the way. I drop my head back and let myself be free for a time to just give my thoughts permission. It's a thing I do sometimes, and something I read in a book, give your thoughts permission. Essentially, let yourself think whatever it might be, no matter how bad, nasty, or naughty it is.

My thoughts go immediately to the moment Brody came on me in the cave. Shit. It's like it is imprinted on my brain now. The other men watching was so erotic.

The way they all vibrated with a barely contained thrum of dark, masculine energy. Something about them screamed to a barely restrained primeval threat of violence. If I'm being utterly honest with myself, I've never felt as powerful as I did in that moment with all those hungry male eyes on me.

Shaking the thoughts off, I sigh and step out of the bath. I can't go there and fall headfirst down this crazy rabbit hole. I just can't. I'll lose myself if I do. I know as much. I need to keep my eye on the prize. The money, and getting enough to find safety for myself, and bring justice knocking on my stepfather's door.

After drying off, I dress in a silky slip of a nightdress that Felicity left for me, and then I take the wine, sipping at more of it, as I head to the present on the side.

I'd quite like something to watch, so pick up the remote for the TV and turn it on.

Moans and skin slapping against skin shock me. I stare at the scene in front of me. What the hell kind of show is this? One woman, and three men, all seemingly serving her every desire. One is sucking on her breast, the other is licking her pussy, and the third her neck.

The sight and sounds go straight to my already desperate desire and ratchet it up more. Shit. I turn over and gape.

What the fuck?

This time it's two women together. They're kissing and squeezing one another's breasts. Is there seriously only porn showing on this television. Is this a joke? A trick played on me by the guys? Or is it part of my treat for winning?

I flick again.

Now I have two men, and oh, my God. I've never actually seen two men fucking. They're beautiful men. Muscular, tan, with smooth, perfect skin. They're lying on a bed that has a gauze curtain billowing in the breeze, and sometimes it covers them so you can only see their vague outline, and others the wind whips it out of the way so you can see everything.

Intrigued, I pause and watch.

One of the men is slowly making love to the other, who is underneath him on his front, arching his back and moaning each time the guy on top drives in.

Damn, it's hot. Really hot.

I rub my neck and wonder if any of the guys have ever done anything like this. My instincts tell me no, and I smirk at the little dip of disappointment I feel.

Sipping at more of the wine, needing the cool liquid to dampen the fire in me, I pull myself out of the trance I'm in and head over to the gift.

Curiosity rising, I take hold of it and tear the paper off.

Okay, they're definitely fucking with me.

It's a smooth, pink vibrator. I turn it over, looking for the switches, but there aren't any. It's a dildo, but obviously not one of the kind that vibrates.

Still, I could work it in and out of myself. My grip on it tightens.

The noise of the men screwing builds, and the wine warms me and slowly takes away my inhibitions.

They won't know, I think to myself. I can use it and then deny it.

Today is a win for me, and I get to treat myself. Those are the rules. Using my new toy will be a nice way to unwind after all the stress.

I turn to go back into the bedroom, but glance at the sofa. I could lie there, where I can see the action on the screen and use this toy.

I shouldn't.

This is giving in to their mind games, and I want to be stronger than that. Then again, what they don't know...

Brody might hate a liar, but is it lying if you simply forget to say anything about it?

I smile and settle on the sofa, carefully placing the wine to one side, on the table, and the toy to the other, on the cushion right by me. As my eyes lift again to the action on the screen, I part my legs and pull my panties to one side. I pick up the dildo and place the tip at my entrance. The smooth silicone is cool against my hot flesh. I'm unsurprised to find that I'm already wet. The scene on screen, combined with the afternoon of being naked, has me hot and bothered.

I'm relieved the dildo is slim and not too long. I've never taken a real cock before, and this toy is a similar size to ones I'd used back home. Anything larger would have been too much. I slide the tip between my folds and then up to circle my clit, before drawing it back down again and dipping it inside me. The silky hem of my nightdress bunches around my hips, and my nipples pebble beneath the shiny material.

I imagine it's two of the guys who are on screen, maybe Rafferty and Brody. Who would be on top out of the two of them? It's hard to pick.

I wonder if any of them took a sneaky peek at me when I'd been naked around the pool. Did they like what they saw? I discovered that I hoped so.

With these thoughts filling my head, and the heavy breathing and groans of pleasure from the television in my ears, I work the dildo deeper. I use my other hand to tease my swollen clit, ratcheting up my arousal so it tightens low in my belly.

Suddenly, the dildo buzzes.

I let out a yelp of surprise and toss it onto the couch. The toy falls silent again.

What the fuck?

Was there a hidden button that I'd hit accidentally? I thought I'd checked it carefully, but I must have missed something. On screen, the two gorgeous men continue to fuck, but now my attention is diverted. I pick up the dildo again and examine it with more care. There definitely aren't any...I pause. Something is different. Now there's a tiny red light on the base. I'm sure that hadn't been there before. Or at least it hadn't been on. I'd have noticed, otherwise. It reminds me of something, too, but I can't quite place it.

I squeeze my thighs together, and the pulse of pleasure that thuds through me reminds me that I'm nowhere near done. It's like this entire day has just been one big tease, and I'm being prevented from getting off. It's beyond frustrating.

Maybe the dildo is activated by body heat, or even moisture? It's certainly possible. A lot of stuff around here is high tech, so even if I've never heard of such a thing, it doesn't mean it doesn't exist. It might even be pressure that gets it buzzing. Perhaps it can pick up on how close a woman is to orgasm and adjusts the speed and intensity of the vibrations accordingly.

It occurs to me that if I'm way off with my thinking and such a thing doesn't exist, I should probably patent the idea. That could be my new career once I've won the money—sex toy designer extraordinaire. I could even write stories that are sold with the toys to give my creative side an outlet.

I grin at my flight of fancy and decide to give the dildo—or I guess it's a vibrator now—another try. The men on screen are still hot and heavy. The one on top has his hand wrapped around the throat of the man beneath, and he seems to be loving it.

My clit tingles again, and I allow my thighs to fall apart. Settling back down in the pillows of the couch, I place the vibrator at my entrance and pause. It should have detected the heat of my body by now, if that is what's activating it, but the vibrations don't restart.

With a sigh of pleasure, I push the vibrator deeper, feeling my inner walls clamp around it. Aah, there's the vibration again. It must be the pressure that makes it work, just like I'd suspected. I guess the patent will have to wait for my next great invention.

I adjust my focus to the men on the television again. The camera has shifted position so the whole screen is filled with big, beautiful cocks. I've got a perfect view of the bottom's asshole stretched wide around the girth of the man on top. I spy the ring of rubber around his base. Good. He's wearing a condom. I'm all for people enjoying sex, but it's important it's safe. I remember the condoms in the supply bag the men have given me. Their presence indicates that these men also intend to be safe with me when the time comes.

What would they have done with me if they'd caught me today? How would it have worked? Would they have each taken turns, staying back to let each of their buddies fuck me in turn? How would they have decided who got to go first? Was it a pre-decided thing, or did they just go with what felt right at the time? Or would it have been like an orgy, with them all on me at once? I pictured me beneath them as they cover me with their mouths and hands and cocks. Would they want me to lie there and take it, or would they prefer me to fight them off?

A tight tingling grips my core, and my nipples harden further. *Fight them off.* Now my imagination has them holding me down, just like Brody did on the beach, while I struggle beneath them, and they feast on me anyway. The vibrations inside me increase, and my pleasure builds.

Chapter Twelve
Asher

"HOLY FUCK."

On the wall of security monitors, we're blessed with multiple views of Honor lying back on the couch, her legs spread, while she fucks herself with her present.

It was in the contract. Zero privacy unless we chose to give it to her. She eats what we tell her, wears the clothes that we tell her, and we get to watch her whenever we want.

I don't think she's considered that, however, given her current position.

I tongue the inside of my cheek. My cock is as hard as iron. I'm not adverse to jacking off in front of the others, but I prefer some privacy when we don't have a girl involved.

"It was a good idea of yours, getting her to spend some naked time by the pool," I tell Rafferty approvingly. "Definitely did the job."

He gives a half grin. "It was her idea to spend time by the pool. I just got her to do it with her clothes off."

I glance at Brody. "You still think something's off with her? I think the whole 'I'm a virgin, please don't hurt me' act was exactly that. An act. Look at her. She's a filthy little bitch. I bet it turns her on to make us think she's innocent. It's probably part of some role-playing kink she's into."

Brody swipes his tongue across his lower lip. "Maybe you're right. But if she's acting, she should be in fucking Hollywood. I've normally got a good instinct for these things."

Wilder growls. "Can't innocent girls have fantasies, too?"

I get the feeling he doesn't like the idea of our little Honor being a whore deep down. He's into them innocent and sweet, and we don't get many of that kind around these parts.

"Turn it up a notch," Rafferty instructs me from where he's standing.

We have a remote control on the vibrator Honor is using. She has no idea, of course. She also has no idea that we have a camera embedded in the television screen that she's positioned herself in front of. The whole thing is completely set up, and that she hasn't seen straight through it surprises me.

Or maybe she has, and she knows exactly what she's doing.

I do as Rafferty instructs and turn the intensity of the vibrations up another level. Honor's reaction is instantaneous. She throws her head back and gasps, squirming against the cushions.

I enjoy having this ability to control her pleasure, even though she doesn't know I'm who's doing it. I remain cool, however, not giving away how this is affecting me to the others. I'm the youngest out of all of them—by more than ten years—and, because of that, I keep my guard up. I don't want any of them to see me as some kid who can't hold his own. Not that I do think they'd see me that way. If it wasn't for me, none of us would have found each other, or built this place.

Of course, it's just a cover—and a good distraction—for the main reason we've come together as a group. When I started my search and put out my intentions via the dark net, I hadn't actually thought I would find others who'd been through what I had. So many who've been in our position would prefer to bury ourselves in shame and pretend like none of it ever happened, but that's one thing all four of us have in common. We refuse to be shamed, and we refuse to forget. We'll *never* forget. Even after we've found the person we're after and have our revenge, we'll always remember what he did to us.

Rafferty thinks it's why I am the way I am. I've killed off that part of me that knows how to empathize, so I don't have to feel any more.

He's probably right.

On screen, Honor spreads her legs wider.

"Zoom in," Wilder says, swallowing hard.

I do, using the commands on the keypad to control the camera now, so we can see the pink, swollen flesh of her pussy, the wetness on her thighs. She's using one hand to strum her clit, while the other jams the vibrator deep in her cunt. Dirty little bitch. She's loving every second of this, putting on a show for us. Wilder might think she's clueless, but I think she knows exactly what's going on.

"Fuck me. We should have bought her a bigger one," Rafferty comments.

Wilder grips the front of his jeans. "She can have a bigger one, but it'll be the real thing next time."

Rafferty arches a brow. "That's if she doesn't win again tomorrow."

I twist to eye him curiously. "She won't keep winning, will she? They never do."

Brody winces. "I'm not sure I've ever had one fight quite that hard before. She gave me a proper boot to the balls. It was like she was determined to get away."

"Maybe she really wanted her treat." Rafferty grins.

"She certainly seems to be enjoying it," Brody says. "How about you step things up another notch."

I do as he requests and turn the vibrator up to maximum power. As well as vibrating, it also wiggles. On screen, Honor's blue eyes widen with shock, and her pretty little mouth opens. I picture myself standing over her, pushing my fingers roughly between those lips so she chokes a little. She certainly seems to be enjoying the movie we've put on for her, and I wonder if she's picturing a hand around her throat as well, squeezing tightly enough to constrict her airway and make her heady with the lack of oxygen, but not enough to make her pass out. If she's never experienced such a thing, she will soon—assuming we can fucking catch her, of course.

Her little moans grow louder, and her hips lift to meet her own ministrations. She's fucking herself good and hard with the vibrator now, slipping it almost fully from her body before slamming it back in. Her slender thighs and calves are taut, displaying long lines of muscle. She hasn't needed to use any lube, her body's natural juices keeping her wet enough to prevent any unwanted friction. Fuck. She's got to be one of the hottest things I've ever seen, and I've seen some freaky shit in my time.

From the deepening of the breathing in the room, I don't think I'm the only one to feel this way.

Her whole body trembles, and she arches into a bow, holding the vibrator deep inside her, her head twisted to one side. She bites her lower lip, and her whole face scrunches up as she gives in to her pleasure. I watch her orgasm shudder through her in waves, once, twice, three times, her body jerking with each ripple.

Finally, she slumps into the cushions. Using the remote control, I switch off the vibrator, and she pulls it from her body and drops it to the floor. Her eyes slip shut, and she looks exhausted and sated. She hasn't even bothered to pull down the hem of her silky nightdress, so her swollen, wet pussy is still on display, panties still skewed to one side.

The room has fallen into silence, as though we're all allowing what we've just witnessed to settle.

"Fuck me," Wilder says eventually. "I don't suppose I can go and knock on her door and offer up the real thing?"

Rafferty shakes his head. "That's not in the rules, remember?"

"Screw the rules." Wilder's frustration is evident in his tone. "Didn't we make the rules up? Surely that means we can change them again, if we choose to."

"Not when she's already signed the contract." Rafferty purses his lips. "Besides, isn't this all just part of the fun? When we set off tomorrow, think how desperate we'll be to catch her and how much sweeter it'll be to get a taste of her."

"And if she manages to evade us tomorrow?" I ask.

Rafferty folds his arms over his chest. "Then she'll get her treat again, and we'll make even more of an effort the following day."

Wilder mutters, "If she leaves this fucking island without me knowing what it feels like to have her tight little pussy wrapped around my cock, I'll lose my fucking mind."

Rafferty pats him on the arm. "Chill, Wilder. She won one game, that's all. Don't lose your shit over one game."

I'm with Wilder on this. I want a taste of her, too. Maybe I'll leave her pussy to Wilder, but I'll happily take her ass. I imagine her on all fours with my cock buried deep in her asshole. In that position, I can grab her ponytail and yank her head right back, like a horse in reins, and wrap my fingers around her slender throat. I don't give a shit about this girl, who she is or where she's some from. She's here as a means to an end, and she'll be well rewarded for it.

Fuck, I need to jack off. I'm going to make a mess of myself like some horny teenager if I'm not careful.

I switch off the monitors and get to my feet. "I'm out of here. Got business to attend to."

Brody snorts. "Yeah, bet you have."

I flip him the bird, though it's not like he's wrong, and head out of there.

Chapter Thirteen
Honor

I LET OUT A FRUSTRATED sigh and toss onto my other side. I kick off the sheets and then pull them back up again, unable to get comfortable, despite the size of the bed and the thread count.

I've been doing this for hours now. I'm kicking myself for taking that nap so late in the day because now I can't sleep and it's driving me crazy. I need to be rested for tomorrow since I'm going to be involved in another chase across the island. What kind of performance will I be able to put in if I'm shattered and just want to sleep? The men will catch me within minutes, and I don't even want to think about what they'll do to me.

Something else is playing on my mind. Tomorrow is the day that I should have been arriving for the maid's job, and when the new maid doesn't show up, someone is going to call the cell number I gave them on my application. When they do, my phone is going to start ringing, and the game will be up—quite literally.

I wonder where they took my bag. Would it be in the big office where I'd been brought to meet the men, or was it more likely going to be in one of the staff offices, like maybe Felicity's or one of the other housekeepers? They probably have a staff room somewhere, which I would have been shown if I'd owned up to who I really was.

Would the doors to any of those places be locked? I really have no idea. But I can try to find out.

With my mind made up, I swing my legs out of bed. I don't want to wander the corridors in the tiny slip of a gown that I'm currently wearing, so I change for the stretchy pants and tank top that is now my customary outfit. I don't bother with a bra. If all goes well, it's not as though anyone is going to see me.

I slip my feet into my boots and go to the door. I'm not locked in here, so I open it a crack and peer out into the corridor. Lighting has been left on, so though it's dark outside, it's bright in here. A part of me wishes for the shelter of darkness.

I give myself a shake. It's not as though I've been told I'm not allowed to leave. No one has said to me that once I'm in my room, I have to stay here. I think of my afternoon around the pool and how I was given free rein of the resort. I'm not a prisoner here, I remind myself. I can leave at any time.

Even so, I still feel as though I'm doing something wrong.

I hurry down the hallway, not one hundred percent sure where I'm going. Do I head up and see if I can get into the men's office, or go down and try to find some kind of staff room where Felicity might have taken my bag?

My heart knocks out a tribal beat against the inside of my ribcage, and my hands shake. If anyone asks what I'm doing, I'll just say I couldn't sleep and so I'm stretching my legs. If I find the bag, I don't even need to take it, necessarily. Just switching the phone off will be enough to stop it from ringing if someone were to call it.

A part of me still feels like taking it, however. It *is* mine, and I don't ever recall reading something in the contract that said I gave them the right to take my belongings. I must admit, though, it's not as though I read the contract properly. I barely gave it a glance before I signed my name—my fake name—on the dotted line. That had probably been a mistake on my part, but I'd been blindsided by the amount of money on offer and the realization that they thought I was someone else. This massive, utterly unexpected opportunity had landed in my lap, and I was worried that, if I'd hesitated, it would have been snatched away again just as quickly.

I wonder what has happened to the girl who is supposed to be in my place. Has she chickened out? I hope so. If she turns up late and I'm taking part instead of her, all hell will break loose. The possibility sends a chill through me. What will the men do if they find out I've been lying about who I am? One thing I know for sure is they definitely won't be happy.

Foregoing the elevators in case I bump into someone inside, I select the door that leads onto the stairwell. All is quiet, and I peer over the edge of the spiral staircase, to the drop below, ensuring no one else is one their way up. So far, so good. I don't know where I'm going yet, and this place is vast. The chance of me locating my belongings is slim, but at least I feel as though I'm being proactive. It's better than lying in bed, worrying and unable to sleep.

Thinking closets and some of the staff quarters are most likely to be on what must be a basement level, a floor below the one I am on, I take the stairs right to the bottom. Sure enough, there's a sign on the door that says, 'staff only.' My pulse quickens. It looks as though my instincts were correct. I wonder if I can claim to be staff if I'm caught—after all, I am technically getting paid.

I push through the door and take in my surroundings. I'm in another corridor, only this one doesn't have the thick, bouncy carpet and expensive artwork of the upper floors. I've no idea what time it is, but everything is quiet. The rest of the staff—the cooks and cleaners and porters—must all be sleeping.

Hurrying down the corridor, I check each door I pass for any sign that one might be an office. The doors are numbered, but in front of each number is the letter 'B.' I assume it stands for basement and is the way these rooms are distinguished from the guest rooms.

I reach one that has a window in it. This is different. I peep through, but it's dark beyond. Could I be in the right place?

There's only one way to find out, so I try the handle. To my surprise, the door opens, and I stick my hand in and pat along the wall, trying to find the light switch. My fingers hit plastic, and I flick the switch, the room flooding with illumination.

I tense, worried I'll have just turned the light on to find someone lying in bed, but instead I'm faced with a bank of metal lockers, some wooden-slat benches, and rows of coat hangers. To one side is a door that leads onto a women's bathroom and changing room, and on the right is the men's.

Just because I've found the staff room doesn't mean I'll also find my stuff.

I approach the lockers. On the front of each one is a slip of card with a different name written on it. Staff members, I assume. I wonder if Felicity has one. I doubt it. I go along, reading each of the names. Francesco Perez. Linda Darcell. Philip Walker. They go on and on. Do all these people still work here, or have they come and gone and no one has bothered to change out the name cards?

I stop and suck in a breath.

Honor Harper.

I can hardly believe it. A locker with my name on it. Will my bag be in here? There's a good chance, but how am I supposed to get inside? It has a combination lock, but of course no one has given me the code. I've seen a few locks being picked during my time on the street, and someone once showed me a trick to opening a bike lock. It's not as though I'm a criminal, but I definitely hung out with some dodgy types for a while there and thinking that these were skills I needed to learn for my own survival, I paid attention.

Low voices come from outside and my stomach lurches. I freeze, unsure of what to do. I don't recognize them, but it's hard to tell at this volume.

Could it be the men? Or do the voices belong to staff members?

My mind whirrs. Should I stay where I am and hope they pass by? But what if they don't and they come in here, instead? If they're members of the staff, there's a good chance they will.

Maybe they'll keep their mouths shut if they see me—after all, shouldn't there be a certain level of camaraderie among the staff? But then I remember that I'm not technically one of them. I would have been, if I'd told the truth and stuck to my original plan, but instead I've been elevated to the woman who's been given the chance to win a million dollars.

The voices grow louder, and I make a split-second decision and dart for the women's bathrooms. I slip into one of the stalls and close the door behind me, then climb onto the closed lid of the toilet. My heart hammers and a wave of nauseated panic sweeps through me.

The main door to the locker room sweeps open and instantly the voices grow louder. They're both male, and I strain my ears to try to recognize them. One laughs and the other joins in.

"Get what you need. It's late."

"Chill, dude."

I relax a fraction. It's not two of the four men, I can tell that much. I still want them to hurry up and leave me alone. The longer I'm out of my room, the more likely it is I'll be discovered.

A metallic clang reverberates through the air. The sound of a locker door hitting the one beside it. There's another clang as it shuts again, and then the swish of the main door opening and closing.

They've left. I'm alone again.

I give it a moment, and then exhale a shaky breath and climb off the toilet. I'm shaky and lightheaded, but I still haven't done what I'd set out to achieve.

Checking the coast is clear, I step back out into the area where the lockers are and go back to the one I'd identified as mine. I need to refocus and concentrate on getting it open, if I can.

I shake out my fingers and clench and unclench my fists, and pull to mind the memory of being taught how to open one of these locks. First, I roll each of the numbers around so they're all at zero and then pull lightly on the end of the lock that will disengage when the correct code is put in. In theory, there should be more of a resistance when I turn the correct dial, so I do exactly that, spinning each of the dials until I feel the resistance in the furthest one. Okay, that must be the one I need to focus on first. I turn that dial slowly, paying attention to how it feels. Just as had been described to me, one of the numbers seems to click into place, like a hole it catches in. Now I go back to the other dials and repeat the process until I have four different numbers selected, four-three-eight-one.

The lock pops open, and I prevent myself whooping in glee. I genuinely hadn't expected it to work—and certainly not so quickly.

Fresh nerves slip through me, wrapping around my lungs and shortening my breath. I might have unlocked it, but that doesn't mean I'll find my bag inside. I could have just wasted my time. I won't know until I check.

I ease open the locker door and bump the air with my fist. My bag is nestled inside. I tug it out and carry it to one of the benches. Upon opening the rucksack, I'm surprised by the wave of sadness that sweeps over me. Not just sadness…nostalgia. It's not my time on the streets I'm missing, or even my time at home, which has been nothing short of hell over these past few years. It's nostalgia for the person I could have become. I've had very little control over the direction my life has taken. Yes, I decided to run, but what were my options? Staying with a man I believed murdered my mother and who was making it clear he planned for me to take her place? I'd tried to report my suspicions to one of his colleagues, but I hadn't been taken seriously. I don't think my report was ever even filed. Instead, I was treated like a hysterical little troublemaker and warned that anything I did or said would backfire on me.

With a sigh, the jubilation I'd experienced at breaking into the locker and finding my bag swiftly retreating, I delve deeper into the bag, searching for my phone. My fingers touch something smooth and thin, and I instantly know what it is. A part of me doesn't even want to look, knowing it'll only solidify the depression weighing heavy in the center of my chest, but not looking feels like a betrayal in itself.

I pull out the photograph of me with my mother, and tears gather in the corners of my eyes. I was about fourteen in this photo, and she would have been about thirty-five. We both look impossibly young and happy. It was taken before *he* had come into our lives. I got my blue eyes from her, but her coloring is lighter, so I can only assume my dark hair and pale skin came from my father. I don't actually know. I've never seen a photograph of him. All I know is his name was David, and he was older than Mom when they'd met. She'd met him playing pool, and he'd bought her a drink, and they'd spent a weekend together. Then he'd vanished, and she'd never heard from him again, and a few weeks later, she'd realized she'd missed her period. I'd never bothered trying to look for him. I didn't exactly have much to go on. Sometimes, I'd wondered if he would have liked to have known about me, to have me in his life, but the feeling is fleeting. He could have been married, for all I know, and would have been horrified to have the offspring of a fling dropping into his life.

I shake off the memories, deposit the photo back in the pack, and resume my search for the phone. I find it right at the bottom and check the screen. The battery only has about twenty percent left on it, so it will be dead in a day or two anyway. I don't have any missed calls or messages, but that doesn't surprise me. No one has this number, except for this place, and they won't have been tracking me down just yet.

Holding my finger down on the button, the phone powers down. I breathe a sigh of relief and drop it back into my bag. A part of me wants to take the bag with me, but if I do, questions will be asked. Instead, I put it back where I found it, click the lock back in place, and mess up the combination code again, covering my tracks.

Chapter Fourteen
Honor

I MANAGED TO GET A few hours' sleep once I'd switched off the phone and got back to my room, unseen. My fear of getting caught in my lie had clearly been playing on my mind more than I'd realized. I still might get found out, of course. There are a lot of different players in this, and I can't control all the variables. Still, I've taken care of the one thing I can control, and that makes me feel better.

The morning has dawned bright and warm once more. I'm in a perfect setting, but darkness has settled around me. My stomach churns at the knowledge a new hunt starts today. I wonder what the prize will be if I win. Set of crotchless panties? Blow up doll? I roll my eyes at the thought, trying to reduce my fear with a bit of sarcasm.

The queasy roiling in my stomach is truly something. Today won't be like yesterday. I'm tired. I have another hunt to endure today. Another day of running from these men. Of wondering what will happen if they catch me. Another day of partly fearing it and partly wanting it.

I sigh and roll over, hugging the pillow for a moment. Then I drag myself out of bed. A fog is hanging over me, and I hope I can shake it. I need to be sharp to stay safe.

I pull my hair back and shower, letting the hot water run over my face in the hope of waking myself up fully. By the time I get out, brush my teeth, and rinse and spit, I'm feeling better. I dutifully apply the scent given to me to use, and dress in the outfit I'm starting to become accustomed to.

Felicity comes to my door to ensure I'm ready for the next game.

"They want to have breakfast with you this morning," she announces.

She doesn't need to define who 'they' are.

I gulp. "Why?"

Her eyes narrow. "Just get a move on. Don't question their motives."

I think perhaps that's exactly what I should be doing. I haven't spent any time with the men since they dropped me off at the resort yesterday. I wonder how they fill their time. Do they have jobs outside of this place? What about families? I realize I know nothing about them. Maybe that's a good thing. The less I know, the less I'll care. All I need to do is last out the next four days, and then I'll be out of here with their check in my pocket, and I'll never need to think about them again.

That'll be easier said than done, especially if they catch me. If I end up being fucked by all four of them by the end of the week, I doubt I'll be able to put what happens out of my mind quite so easily.

Guilt and shame work their way through me. They're effectively paying to fuck me. I guess that makes me a whore.

I've definitely never thought of myself in such a way before—for fuck's sake, I'm still a virgin. If I'd had any idea this was what lay in my future, I would have taken the jump a whole lot sooner. I wish I had at least a little experience behind me right now. I wonder which of them will be the first to take me. Rafferty seems to be the boss, and the eldest of the group. The thought of it being Wilder is frankly terrifying, considering the size of him. I've already had some experience of being intimate with Brody—he's the one that I've had the most contact with so far. He came on me. I've seen his cock. I've kicked him in the balls. It's quite the history he and I are making.

As for Asher...well...him, I'm not sure about. He looks harmless on the outside, and he's closer to me in age, and not huge like Wilder. But there's something about him that unnerves me, an edge that he tries to keep hidden.

I shake the thoughts out of my head. None of them are going to take my virginity, and I'm not going to make a whore out of myself, because I simply won't let them catch me.

Felicity leads me to a room I haven't been in before, and as I enter, I discover I'm in a formal dining hall. All four men are already here. A buffet-style setup of breakfast food is along one wall, and the familiar scent of coffee and bacon fills my senses. My stomach contracts, and I realize how hungry I am.

"Good morning, Honor," Rafferty says from where he stands at the buffet. He's being formal, as usual. "We thought you might like to join us this morning."

"Oh...umm...thanks."

He gestures to the food. "Help yourself. Whatever you want."

I sense the eyes of the others on me. They're all eating, but their attention is directed my way. I clock what's on each of their plates. Wilder has a giant pile of bacon, eggs, and hashbrowns. Rafferty has what appears to be eggs Benedict—given away by the creamy yellow sauce. Brody has smoked salmon on a thick rye bread, and Asher has large mushrooms with wilted spinach. His plate interests me the most. No meat, eggs, or even fish? Is Asher vegan?

Self-conscious, I approach the food, pick up a spare plate, and place some lightly scrambled eggs and smoked salmon onto it. I'll need my strength for the day ahead, but I'm not sure how easily I'll be able to eat if they all keep staring at me like that. What the hell is going through their minds? Are they thinking about the day's hunt, or has something else got them all het up?

I take my plate to the spare seat that's the farthest from them all, sit down, and start to eat. The scrambled eggs are creamy and light, and the smoked salmon melts in my mouth. I should be enjoying this, especially after living on crap for the past couple of months, but I have a horrible sensation the men know something I don't.

I continue to eat, but the food has lost all taste. I'm just waiting for them to give me the instructions for the day's game.

Asher pushes back his chair and gets to his feet. He works his way around the table, in my direction, and pauses behind me.

He speaks low in my ear. "Hey, baby girl. How'd you like your present?"

I duck away and blush. "I wouldn't know. I didn't bother to open it."

It's a stupid lie. One look in my room and they'll see that I have.

"Really?" I can hear the amusement in his tone. "I thought you might have had fun last night."

I immediately balk. "What do you mean?"

"Getting some time to yourself? What is it people call it these days? Self-care?"

I blinked rapidly. The son of a bitch is talking about the vibrator. Obviously, they know what the prize was, but I hadn't been expecting them to ask me about it the following day. Can't a girl have a little privacy?

"I haven't heard that expression," I lie. "What does it mean?"

"Oh, you know, the bubble bath and good food? Did you like the wine we provided?"

I relax a fraction. Maybe he isn't asking about the sex toy. I'm just being paranoid. Then again, I have every reason to be paranoid. At least he hasn't asked about what I'd been up to in the middle of the night.

There's an odd atmosphere in the room. One that hasn't been here before. The way they all seem somewhat on edge, except for Asher, who is like the cat who got the cream for some reason.

Rafferty steps forward and slides a folded piece of paper onto the table beside my half-eaten food. My hand trembles as I reach out and pull it toward me. My breakfast churns in my stomach.

I unfold it and quickly scan the contents. My experience yesterday means I'm able to easily pick our current location and then spot the X they've marked off on it. It's nowhere near where we were the previous day.

Realizing this is his way of telling me breakfast is over, I fold the map back up and rise from my seat. I clutch the map tightly, hoping the sweat trickling from my palms doesn't smear the ink.

"Okay, your backpack." Rafferty hands me the pack. "You don't get as big a head start today, as the ground you have to cover isn't so far to this prize. However, it is tricky. You're going in the opposite direction, and you need to be careful, okay? There are some areas where the vegetation is quite overgrown. Don't go falling."

My tone is laced with sarcasm. "Ah, you care. How sweet."

"There's some extra stuff in your backpack today, including a waterproof bag for you to put your clothes in."

"Why?"

"The last part of the journey means swimming from one cove to the next."

"Can't I just go around?"

"You can, but *we* won't be. If you want to get to the end only to find us already there, waiting for you, then, by all means, go the long way."

He stares at me, challenging.

I relent. "Okay, fine."

"It's only a short swim," he continues, "but you can't get your clothes wet."

"Why not?"

"Because we said so, and besides, you'll need to redress when you reach the other side."

"Wait, you want me to swim and carry my backpack?"

He nods, but then shrugs. "Or you can leave it all on the beach and return for it once you find the prize. It just means you'll be naked while you complete the rest of the hunt."

"I like naked," Wilder supplies.

So did I when I was by the pool, but I'm thinking that climbing through bushes, and crawling over rocks, all while being attacked by small biting creatures is probably better done with some clothes on.

"Wait a minute. Can't I wear my underwear to swim in?"

Rafferty's blue gaze hardens. "No. You swim naked. Those are our rules, and you have to abide by them. Got it?"

"Fine," I snap, as if I'm so over it all.

He merely grunts, shoves the backpack at me, then taps the face of his expensive watch. "Time's a-ticking, darling. Get moving."

I want to slap him. Instead, I give him what I hope is a sardonic smile, and, resisting the urge to flip them all the bird, I take off.

I'm fully aware of the ticking clock, and that I need to put as much distance between me and them as possible. It was close yesterday—if it wasn't for that well-timed kick to Brody's balls, they would have caught me. I hope the bastard is still suffering. I move at a jog through the building. I don't want to set off too fast for fear of running out of steam too quickly. That they can keep changing the amount of head start I get is frustrating. What if one of these days they decide not to give me a head start at all? I'd barely have the chance to get out of the building.

I burst out of the main doors of the resort and take off across the manicured grounds. According to the map, I need to be heading toward the cliffs, but there's a good distance to cover before I get there. I leave the hotel and pool and beaches behind and strike out across the island.

Insects buzz around my head, and I slap at the bare skin of my arms each time I feel the tickle of tiny legs. I don't have the cover of shade from trees like I did yesterday. The sun glares down on my head, and I pause long enough to pull open the backpack and delve inside for supplies.

I work quickly, slapping sun lotion onto my exposed skin, all the while glancing over my shoulder to ensure no one is coming. I locate a baseball cap, which I jam on over my head to prevent my face and scalp getting burned, and then a bottle of water that I take a long draw from. In this heat, it'll be easy to become dehydrated, and I know that'll be a bad thing. Dehydration can kill, but before that, it'll cause headaches and dizziness and fatigue.

If I get dizzy and tired, I'll make mistakes.

I do the bag back up, hook it back over my shoulders, and keep going.

Ninety minutes in, I realize Rafferty wasn't wrong when he said this was harder terrain. It's rocky, uneven, and full of bushes and scrub. I go over on my ankle twice, cursing as I do. At this rate, I'm going to rupture a tendon or something.

Pausing, I take the water back out of my bag and gratefully chug it down. I examine the map. I need to head east from where I am. I figure it will take me another twenty minutes to reach where I need to be for the short swim to the next cove. I might have a chance to win again.

Wouldn't it be something if I won every game, and got the million without having to do anything sexual?

BLURRED LIMITS

I'm shocked at the sharp twinge of dismay my thought produces.

I shake my head at myself. "You don't want them, Honor. This is just about the money. Don't go getting all Stockholm Syndromey."

Is that even a thing? I doubt it.

I'm back into a steady jog when I stop to get my bearings for a moment. The swell of surf hitting the shore greets my ears. I grin. Oh, my God, I am going to do it. Again.

Yes!

I race down to the beach. I strip my clothes off, but rebelliously leave my underwear on. Rafferty might have said it was dangerous to swim clothed, but my bra and panties is basically just a bikini. I recognize the 'rule' for what it is—a pretty thin excuse to get me naked.

I'm not a bad swimmer, but I'm not the best, and I don't relish dragging the backpack with me full of my clothes, boots, and supplies. I don't have far to go once I've swum to the other side, so I'll do the rest barefooted and in my underwear, and the minute I've claimed the next prize, I'll haul ass back here and get dressed again. I place everything in the pack, zip it, and leave it to one side. Then I head to the water.

I step in and, as I wade deeper, the cold hits me. Wow, it's not warm as you get farther out. I take in a deep breath and dive in. Might as well get it over with.

Cold has me gasping in shock as I surface. I turn myself in the water until I am facing the correct way and then I swim for my life.

It only takes around five minutes to get around the narrow promontory and to the next cove.

As I clamber out of the water, I take a look around me. The little natural bay is stunningly beautiful. It's the sort of place that would make for a lovely romantic rendezvous. Not that I'll be getting that. No, I'll be finding myself taken by four fucked-up, and probably highly dangerous, men if they catch me.

"Hey there, pretty little thing."

My blood freezes, at the same time my heart kicks into rapid gear. Shit.

I whip around. Rafferty smiles at me as I stare in shock. How the fuck did he get here first? How come I didn't see him? Where has he come from?

I glance all around, looking for the others, but there's only him.

"Just you and me right now, princess," he states. "Today, you lose."

Chapter Fifteen
Rafferty

HER FACE IS A PICTURE. She's nervous, scared, confused, and maybe a little excited. I don't get Brody's issue with her. I think she's fairly easy to read. A proverbial open book. All the things she feels rush across her face like clouds across a summer sky.

She's so pretty. Delicate, too. That makes me want to hurt her more. My palms itch to smack her ass and thighs. I hold myself in check. This is only game two. Can't go giving her the full Asher treatment quite yet. If I do, we have no stakes to raise. Still, I want some fun time without the others.

She shakes her head and takes a step back. "No, no, no, no."

She goes to dart away, most likely hoping to put some distance between us, but I'm faster, and I grab hold of her wrist. I remember how she kicked Brody in the balls yesterday, and I don't want to give her the same opportunity again. I yank her in against my body, so her back is to my chest, and lock my arm around her, my forearm crushing her breasts, preventing her from moving.

Honor lets out a yell of frustration and fights against me, her small, lithe body squirming. She's half naked and dripping wet, and having her struggle against me like this is making me hard. I buck my hips forward, so my burgeoning erection jams into the small of her back. I ensure she knows exactly what she's doing to me.

She flinches and instantly falls still.

What the hell? She's supposed to be into this stuff as much as we are, but there are moments where she makes me wonder.

My grip tightens.

"You do as you're bid, understand?" My tone is serious. "You lost."

She swallows and makes a sound somewhere between a squeak and a sob.

"This way."

Only a few minutes farther down this path is an old hut. We kept it for our fun and games. Now I want to play with her in there. I should really wait for the others to find us, but I don't want to. I could have some fun out here on the beach, but in there are some extra props.

I release her enough that she can walk but stands no chance of breaking free. Honor stumbles twice, and I steady her each time. She seems a little off her game today. A flashback to her pussy all wet and needy as she shoved the vibrator inside hits me. No wonder she's exhausted. She overexerted herself last night. I laugh, and she swings her head my way.

"What are you laughing at? This isn't funny."

"Nothing," I lie. "Something I thought about."

She doesn't push it further, but she looks up and sees the hut. Her bare heels dig into the ground, effectively halting us both, and she twists in my grip. "What is this? What are you doing?"

I'm getting impatient. "Jesus, Honor, what is it with you? You know the fucking rules. You love playing the scared little mouse, don't you?"

"Maybe I *am* the scared little mouse."

"Maybe."

I push open the door and hit the light switch. I shove Honor inside and close the door by kicking it shut with the back of my heel.

She crosses her arms over her chest while I admire her body. She's got great curves. Nice, fairly big, natural tits. Narrow waist, flaring out to lovely hips, and then slender legs. She's petite, and scared, and all wet, and I'm about right out of patience.

"Take your clothes off," I demand.

"I haven't got any on."

"Your underwear." I harden my tone. "Take. It. Off."

She looks around the room as if the walls can somehow help her. God, she's adorable. We're going to fuck her up so bad.

"If I refuse?" she says.

"Then I'll tear it off your fucking body. Trust me when I tell you I'm giving you the easier route."

Slowly, her hands trembling, she unfastens the bra and lets it drop to the ground. I've seen her pussy before, but it doesn't stop my mouth watering when she pushes her panties down her legs and kicks them to one side. She's naked, and I want to cover every inch of her skin with my hands, my mouth, my tongue. I want to consume every inch of her until it's impossible to tell where I end and she begins.

I move so fast I doubt she sees me coming. I have her up against the wall with my hand around her throat before she can react. Her eyes are wide as she stares at me. I push her head up, and then force my thumb into her mouth.

"I told you to be naked when you swam, didn't I?"

She nods, her head barely moving because of the vise I'm holding her in.

"Next time I tell you something, you do it. Okay?"

Another tiny nod.

I take my thumb from her mouth, and she releases it with a satisfying little pop. Letting one finger trail down between her breasts, I smile. "Wet."

She swallows, and her throat bobs against my palm.

"Are you wet everywhere, Honor?"

I let my fingers trail over her stomach, down, farther down, until I'm parting her folds. She whimpers when I push my way between them with my middle finger.

Victory races through my blood when I find out she is wet. Very. I lift my finger away and suck it into my mouth, the taste of her exploding on my tongue.

If her eyes get any wider, she's going to look like a cartoon character.

The door bursts open, and Wilder strolls in all casual-like, followed by Asher, and bringing up the rear, Brody.

Asher narrows his eyes. "Starting without us?"

"Always. You guys should have been faster."

"Fuck you," he replies.

I decide to assert some authority over him, too. "Go get the spreader bar," I order. "And the cuffs."

He narrows his eyes but does as I say, cursing under his breath as he stomps to the chest in the corner of the room.

"Cuffs?" Honor squeaks.

I walk her roughly over to the couch, stand her behind it, and hold her in place while Asher takes his sweet time finding what I asked for.

She struggles beneath me. "No, wait. Stop."

Her pleas make me hard. She knows the safeword if she really wanted this to end. It's all part of the game.

When he comes back, I fix the spreader bar to her ankles, so her legs are nicely spread. Then I cuff her wrists in front of her.

My breathing is choppy because this is turning me on a lot more than our games normally do. I'm not sure if it's because she is supposedly a virgin, or if it's because there's a delicious mix of defiance and fear swirling around inside her. At the end of this day, this is all roleplay, but for some reason, with her, it feels real.

I shove her over the back of the couch. "Stay," I order with my palm resting firmly on her back.

Then I step back and admire my handiwork.

Hands in front of her, out straight, her body is bent double at the waist where she's draped over the couch. As her legs are spread, it means her pussy is exposed to the four of us. Her teeth are clenched, as though she'd has the safeword clamped between them.

"Nice," Wilder says appreciatively.

"She broke the rules," I tell them. "I said swim naked, but she had her underwear on."

"That's not good," Brody rumbles. "You break the rules this early on, how can we expect you to ever stick to them? We need to teach you a lesson." He turns to me. "Let me do the honors."

I smirk at his play on words. "Go at it."

He walks up to her and runs his middle finger down the back of her thigh. She trembles, and I lick my lips.

The first crack of palm against flesh rings out in the room but is drowned out by her astonished cry of pain.

Brody hits her again, and again. Each blow is measured, and pretty restrained, but Honor is making a lot of noise in response.

"Shut up," Brody orders. "Or I'll stop going easy on you."

"Easy?" She turns to try to look behind her. "This isn't sex. This is...this is painful."

"It's sex for us," I tell her drily.

"Make her ass pink," Asher demands, his voice gruff.

"My pleasure."

Brody really gets to work. He spanks her fast and rhythmically until she's got a nice red glow to each perfect cheek. Each time his palm makes contact with her skin, she jerks forward and lets out a sexy little yelp.

Honor squirms against the sofa, and I don't think it's in lust. She really doesn't like the spanking.

Tough. We do, and today is our day. We won. She lost.

"There, see?" Brody says to her. "You took it like a good girl."

"You're sick," she whispers.

"Oh, if you think we're sick from this, you've got a shock coming your way," I reassure her. "Guess what?"

She speaks from between gritted teeth. "What?"

BLURRED LIMITS

"You didn't hate it as much as you think you did."

"What do you know?"

"You're even wetter." I drag my finger through her folds once more and hold it up for the other guys. Then I grab her hair and pull her head up. "Lick it off," I demand.

She stares at me, and I swear there's something akin to real hatred there for a moment. Then she darts out her perfect pink tongue and licks my finger clean.

I want to shove my dick down her throat, but I'm a master of restraint, of playing the long game. I have no issue with delayed gratification, so I don't. Anyway, today, I want her to see Wilder's cock. She doesn't have to take it in her pussy today, but she needs to see it so I can watch her reaction.

The other guys don't know it, but I've got a voyeuristic streak a mile long, and I love seeing how women react to Wilder's monster dick.

"You lick things very well," I say mildly. "Wilder, would you like her to lick something of yours?"

He grins. "Why, I think I would."

Asher laughs, and even Brody smirks.

"Brody, why don't you come and take a closer look at this lovely pussy?"

He grins at me. "Yes, sir."

Then he comes and kneels right behind Honor, his face millimeters from her ass and pussy.

He blows on her, and she jumps, her thighs shaking.

I want to watch from the front. I want to see her face when she first gets a good look at what Wilder is packing.

I move around the sofa and watch intently as Wilder kneels on it, right in front of her. Because she's bent over the back of it, to lift her head, she has to place her cuffed hands on the sofa seat and hold herself up a little. It's awkward for her, which only adds to the pleasure of it for me, and Asher, too, I'm sure.

Wilder isn't as sadistic as the rest of us. He just gets off on making them take his huge dick.

He unzips his pants and reaches in. He'll be going commando, if I know him. Sure enough, a moment later, he pulls his giant appendage straight out.

Honor stares, blinks, and then the color drains from her face.

He's got to be at least nine inches, maybe ten, but he's thick too, like a fucking beer can. Then right at the end, shining in the dim light streaming in through the dusty window, is his piercing.

He shakes his dick at her as if to introduce it to her, and she gulps.

When she looks up at me, it's with genuine fear in her eyes. Oh, yeah, she's figuring out she's got to accommodate that in her pussy at some point.

"Don't worry, Snow." Wilder strokes her cheek. "We aren't doing that today, and when we do, you'll be good and ready."

For a moment, my legal sense of responsibility reasserts itself, and I turn Honor's face up with my thumb. "This all gets too much, do you remember your word?"

She nods.

"Good."

Wilder taps her cheek with his dick. "You ever sucked a pierced dick before?"

She shakes her head.

BLURRED LIMITS

"This first time, I'll go easy on you. Don't want to damage your precious little throat."

He didn't just go for something easy like a Prince Albert, no Wilder made his already scary dick way more so by having an apadravya bar straight through it. The piercing is specially designed to hit a woman's G-spot, and I've personally watched it at work. Any woman riding Wilder's huge, pierced cock is likely to lose her mind. There's a part of me that's just a little jealous.

"You can start by just licking it if you're scared," Wilder says, the fucking freak. He gets off on this so bad.

Worse, I get off on watching it. Something I've never examined too closely.

Honor makes a strange sound in the back of her throat, something akin to a hum crossed with a whimper, and then she sticks her pointy little tongue out and licks up Wilder's shaft.

His eyes drift closed for a moment as she licks up and down the shaft. She said she's never licked a pierced dick before, but the way she's acting, it's like she's never sucked cock. Is it all part of her 'innocent little girl' act? I have to admit, she's good at it, and I fucking like it.

"Lick the head," I tell her, my voice hoarse. God damn, what the fuck is wrong with me with this girl?

Her eyes dart to mine for a moment, and then she stares back at the cock bobbing in front of her face like some massive fucking snake. She licks his head, her tongue curling around the bar and then swiping the slit in the middle. Wilder weeps some pre-cum.

"Clean it up like a good girl," Asher orders.

She licks the clear liquid, and Wilder immediately produces some more. It seems I'm not the only one turned on beyond belief.

She licks that too, and halfway through doing so, she opens her mouth and cries out.

I turn to look behind her, and see that Brody is on his knees and has buried his face in her pussy and is eating her out like she's an all you can eat buffet and he's been starving for months.

"Make sure you don't bite me, darling," Wilder chuckles.

Soon, the sounds and scents of sex fill the room. Brody worships Honor's pussy while she tries to lick and suck on Wilder's cock.

"You need to take him in your mouth," I order her. I undo my own zipper, slide my pants down to my knees, and push my underwear down too. Taking my cock in hand, I turn her face to me.

"Here, sweetheart, practice on me first."

She opens her mouth to say something, but I don't give her chance. I shove my dick in deep. Her throat closes around me reflexively, and damn, it feels good. Hot and wet.

She splutters, and I pull out a little, before thrusting straight back in the moment she seems to have some control over herself.

"Just relax. You don't need to do anything but relax."

Soon, I've got a rhythm going, fucking that perfect, innocent face, and I know I won't last long. Pleasure condenses in my balls, and my thighs, ass, and stomach tense. I chase my orgasm, pumping harder and faster, uncaring for if she might be struggling. I'm right on the edge, and as I topple over the brink, I grab her hair in a tight fist so I can hold myself deep without her pulling away. When I come, it's with a hoarse shout as I empty down her fluttering throat.

"There you go," I say as I finally pull out. "You're all nice and lubed up now to try to take Wilder."

Her eyes are full of tears, and I don't know if they're purely physical from choking on my dick, or emotional.

I tell myself not to care. It's not as if she can't tap out anytime she wants. One word, that's all it takes, and this ends.

"Your turn, I think." I gesture to Wilder.

"I need to come," Asher states. "Undo her hands, I want them on me."

I do as he says, unfastening the cuffs around her wrists.

It's not going to work, her trying to use her hands on Asher while she's bent over the sofa.

Fuck it. I undo the spreader bar too, freeing her legs, then I throw her over my shoulder and march out of the door. The guys follow me, one after the other, Wilder grabbing a throw from the back of a chair. The bright sunlight hurts my eyes for a moment, but I soon adjust.

Carefully, I lower Honor to the ground and place her on the throw Wilder puts down. Brody immediately falls between her legs, pushing them roughly apart so he can go back to eating her pussy.

Wilder straddles her and pushes his massive dick down to her mouth, pressing her jaw with his thumb and forefinger to make her open up. Asher takes one of her hands and wraps it around his dick, and they use her while I watch and get hard all over again.

Chapter Sixteen
Honor

The safeword is on the tip of my tongue. It reverberates through my mind, repeatedly. I am on the edge of saying it because this...degradation can't be happening.

The money stops me.

The money and something else. Something I don't want to admit to. Something deep and dark stirring within me.

I have a dick in my hand, and another shoved in my mouth, and this one is so thick my jaw aches even though Wilder hasn't made me take him deep the way that bastard, Rafferty, did.

Then as if that weren't enough, Brody is sucking on my pussy, and I can feel my orgasm building, even as I don't want to come for him. This needs to end. I just want it to stop. I also want it to last forever because Wilder's dick tastes amazing, and holding Asher all hot and heavy in my hand makes me feel powerful. I discover I want to bring each and every one of them to their knees. Brody's tongue is legit magic, and I think he's got to be some kind of wizard or sex-deity because surely no mortal man can do the things he is.

The bar through Wilder's dick catches in my mouth and the back of my throat every now and again, and I imagine what it will be like in my pussy. Scary. I bet it will hurt.

Brody sticks two fingers inside me, gentle at first, but then he pumps them harder. Oh, shit. I can't hold off any longer, I'm going to come. I know it as much as I know the sun is going to set in a few hours.

I dig my nails into the sand below me as my body straightens. My other hand manages to keep some kind of rhythm going for Asher, but I'm not sure how.

My back bows, and I cry out as the most intense orgasm I've ever had overtakes me. Brody lashes my clit with his tongue, and my pussy contracts and releases repeatedly, squeezing his fingers tight.

"Holy shit, Pan, you're going to be a tight fuck if I ever manage to get my cock inside you," Brody snarls as if the idea makes him angry.

As I start to come back to a semblance of reality, Wilder grunts, and my mouth fills with copious amounts of salty fluid.

I try to swallow but start to splutter. He pulls out and finishes coming all over my lips.

Then Asher finds his own release, hips jerking into my hand as he comes, too.

Wilder takes me completely by surprise when he grips my face in one of his big hands and kisses me hard. I wasn't expected to be kissed. That's not what this is about, surely?

"You were amazing," he says, a softness to his voice, and he clambers off me.

Brody slips his fingers from my pussy and then sits up enough to drag his t-shirt over his head. Something metal catches in the sunlight, and I realize those are military ID tags he's wearing. So, Brody has a military background—maybe he's

BLURRED LIMITS

even still serving, and this is how he spends his time off. I like that I know something about him now.

I struggle to sit, my chest heaving. Rafferty is standing a few feet away from where my soles rest on the sand. He's staring at me, thinking.

Oh, God, isn't it over?

"You think she's ready for a cock?" he asks Brody, "or we should save that for tomorrow?"

"Well, what if she wins tomorrow?" Brody answers. He cocks his head to one side as if he's considering a serious philosophical question. "If we don't win tomorrow, that only leaves us a couple more games, and we need to take her ass as well, and then she's got to take more than one of us...I say we take her pussy now."

My ass? What the hell? Oh, no. Nope. No way in hell. And two of them?

"She's all wet and ready," Brody says with a grin. "I did good prep work for you."

"*She* is here," I snap.

"Yeah, and *she* doesn't get a say, unless it's a certain word, so shut the fuck up," Asher replies.

I stare at him, hurt. He carried me on the first day. Sometimes I feel as if I've made a breakthrough with him, but then he's cold and harsh with me. The man gives me whiplash.

"Why don't you do it, Rafferty, but do it nice. Just for her first time." Brody's words have a hint of sarcasm to them.

Doesn't he believe I'm a virgin?

Rafferty grins and strips off his clothes. Asher reaches for a backpack he's got with him and rifles through it. He grabs a condom pack and tosses it to Rafferty, who expertly catches it.

When Rafferty's fully undressed, I can't help but stare. He could be that actor who plays Superman. He's classically handsome, with a perfect, sculpted physique. He's not as big as Wilder, but he's strong, and full of muscle and long, lean sinew. He looks like an Olympic swimmer, whereas Wilder simply looks like a giant.

Rafferty wasn't lying when he said they sunbathe naked, because he's got a light tan, and it is *all* over. He has tattoos, too, and I notice one of them is the same as the one Wilder has –the triangle with the eye in the middle. Do they all have it tattooed on their bodies? I'm far too distracted right now to start questioning him about what it means.

His cock is hard again, although he came only recently.

He's big but not monstrously so like Wilder.

He rips the condom packet with perfect white teeth, takes it out, and rolls it slowly down his length. I watch, fascinated, unable to tear my eyes away.

Shit, this is really happening. They are really going to take my virginity, or at least, Rafferty is. I never wanted things to go this far. I'd gotten cocky. I thought I was going to keep winning. I was wrong.

Shame fills me, and my cheeks burn, and it's not just because of the hot sun. I've done what I told myself I wouldn't. I've whored myself out. I should stop this now, prevent it from going any farther. But if I do, the million dollars will never be mine. Not only that, I'll have to leave the island. Yes, I'll have some extra money, so at least I won't have to sleep rough anymore, and I'll be able to buy myself some decent meals, but none of those things will prevent my stepfather from finding me. At least here, for the past couple of days, I haven't been

BLURRED LIMITS

looking over my shoulder the whole time. I can't imagine what would happen if my stepfather found me here. How would these four men react? Would they try to protect me, or would they hand me over?

Rafferty drops to his knees beside me and runs a hand up my body. His palm is rough and hot. He palms my breasts and tweaks one nipple hard.

"How do you want it, sweetheart?" He says it as if he really cares, but I can tell this is just a game to them. "Soft and easy for the first time?"

I don't reply. If I say yes, will they laugh and tell me I'm getting it hard.

"Ah, not sure?" Asher says mockingly. "Give it her gentle, Rafferty."

"Yeah, don't want to destroy that virgin pussy before we all get a turn," Brody adds.

I grit my teeth. The thing is, the sex side of it isn't so bad, although I did not like the spanking. But this? The way they talk to me and about me is fucked up. What happened to these men to make them this way? I want to slap them. Or tell them to go fuck themselves. But then I remind myself this is a game. When I won the other day, they treated me with respect, didn't they? The woman they think I am likes it this way. Or at least she was willing to say she did for the money.

I close my eyes and decide to pretend this isn't happening. As I squeeze them shut, a tear runs down the side of my face. Rafferty's hot breath hits my cheek, and then he licks the tear away.

"Oh, no. Eyes on me, sweetheart." Rafferty's words are an order, not a request.

I hitch a breath but do as he says. I look at him as he bends his dark head and takes one aching nipple into his mouth. I try not to react, but my body reaches for him as if it has a life of its own, independent of my brain and what I tell it to do.

He uses some teeth to add a little bite of pain into the mix, and I find, unlike the spanking, I quite like that. He does it again, and a small moan escapes me. I clamp my mouth shut tight but catch Asher's expression. He's smirking like the arrogant fucker he is.

God, this is humiliating with all of them watching me.

Rafferty sucks on my other breast and gives it the same treatment as his hands wander all over my body. He climbs over me and presses his own body to mine, and the feeling is incredible. I've messed about before and done a lot of things, but I've never done this. Skin on skin, completely naked. It feels wonderful. I can see how it could become addictive having a warm, heavy body over mine, protecting me, and at the same time dominating me. It's heady.

He kisses me on the mouth, the way Wilder did, but Rafferty's kiss isn't as hard, and when he swipes my bottom lip with his tongue, I open for him. I taste mint, and Rafferty, and I wonder if he can taste Wilder's cum. The thought excites me. He explores my mouth lazily, while his hands trail all over my flesh, setting it alight, and his body moves against mine in a rhythm that feels as if we're already making love.

His thighs nudge mine farther apart, and I comply. He breaks off his kiss and looks at me, deep in the eyes. His gaze holds mine. "This might hurt at first," he says, and for once he seems serious. "If you really are a virgin, this will hurt, but it won't be for long."

Then he pushes into me, and at first it feels nice, like with the dildos I've used, but as he goes deeper, I screw my face up and hold my breath. Okay. That does hurt. I'm not controlling the angle or the speed, and when I play with my toys, I never go this far with them. He's hitting something deep, and little darts of pain shoot through me, and then there's a shift in position and it feels tight. I give a little groan of pain.

Rafferty stills. "Breathe, don't hold your breath."

I do as he says and suck in some air.

It helps, and for a moment I relax, but then he really starts to move, and the pain isn't the problem anymore. It's that this feels really, really good. Like the vibrator but so much better. He's set up a smooth rhythm, and every now and again he changes the angle, and then he hits something in me, and I squeal. Oh, God, what was that? It's like too much. Too amazing. I push against the sand with my heels as if I can get away from it.

"Oh, no you don't," he murmurs as he grabs my hands and pins them to the sand.

He hits that spot again, and again. Each time he slams into me, grazing that part inside me, I see stars, and I am worried I might pass out or something because everything suddenly feels far too intense. I can't do anything except hold on for the ride, and it becomes a wild one when Rafferty snaps his hips and ups the speed.

He slams into me, and I cry out because I am going to come, and I know it's going to make the earlier orgasm look like nothing. Instinctively, I wrap my legs around him, pulling him deeper.

Rafferty looks down at me, and there's something in his gaze I've not seen before. It's triumph and maybe something a little like awe.

He lets go of my wrists, and my arms fly around him, and I hold on to him tight as he pounds me. Every nerve ending in my body is firing, every muscle tensed. I feel as though I'm going to explode and then disintegrate into nothing. And even though I never wanted this, and certainly never wanted to lose my virginity with an audience, I discover I don't want him to stop. I need this more than anything I've ever needed in my life. If he does stop, I fear I might lose my mind.

When it hits, I scream, not caring about all the men surrounding us. I cry out and hold on as I soak Rafferty with my release, coming so hard I sob.

What the fuck? My head drops back on the throw as I bring one arm over my face, covering it as I suck in air. What was that?

Rafferty keeps pumping inside me, and he groans as he finds his own release, the second for him that day.

He rolls off me and kisses me on the forehead as he chuckles. "Well, I think we can safely say you were definitely a G-spot virgin."

"I was the real kind of virgin," I whisper.

"You've not bled," Asher points out.

I sigh at his idiocy. "I've used toys before. And anyway, most girls break their hymen with things like tampons, or even sports activities." I explain the basics to him, and when I glance at him, I regret it.

His face is slightly flushed, and he looks pissed. Oh, great. I don't want to make an enemy of him. I offer him a smile, as if 'hey, look, just joking,' but he doesn't smile back.

"Serious time out. Game's over for now," Rafferty orders as he stands and pulls me up.

I try to stand, but my legs are like jelly.

"You were a virgin, for real? Not as part of the game?" he asks as he steadies me.

"For real. I've...you know...with toys, but I've never been with a man before." Then I glance at him from under my lashes. "You were my first."

For a moment, it's as if there's a connection between myself and Rafferty.

"Well, shit," Brody says. "Hopefully, I'll get my turn tomorrow."

And just like that, the spell is broken, and I remember my place in all this.

I'm just the fuck toy.

Chapter Seventeen
Wilder

THE WHOLE WAY BACK to the compound, something twists in my chest, and I don't get it. I'm not jealous of these men. We've played with many women together before, and I've never felt the overwhelming rush of possessiveness I did over Snow when she told Rafferty he'd been her first.

I'd wanted that to be me.

I wanted to see her try to take me for her very first time. I know, logically, that's a bad idea. My dick is massive, and with the piercing, I'd have destroyed her, but it doesn't mean I didn't want it.

She's so beautiful, and the way she responds to us is as if she was made for us. Made for this twisted game we like to play.

I like her, which is kind of new for me. Not that I dislike any of the women we've had here, but it's a casual bit of fun with a dark and fucked-up edge, and then we say goodbye. That's all it ever is. This, however, feels like it could be something more. Trouble is, there are four of us, and one of her, so it could never work, and she leaves in a few days, anyway.

The others don't seem to feel the same. They treat her with the same semi-contempt they reserve for all the girls who do this. There was a moment, though, when he fucked her, where I believe Rafferty maybe felt it, too. It's hard to tell with him. He's not as hard as Brody, or as messed up as Asher, but he's not soft and fluffy either. Sometimes I think he's a bit like a machine. He keeps on going, doing his thing without seeming to feel much of anything.

Honor looks like she's about to drop, and I decide that this time, I want her in my arms. I don't give her a chance to start dressing. I want her naked. Sweeping her up, I ignore her shriek of protest and hold her to me, cradling her warm, small body against mine.

"Oh, my God, what is it with you guys carrying me?" she asks.

"Only polite if we've worn you out," I reply.

"It's a long walk back." She yawns.

"See that gap there, where the beach turns into trees at the far end?" I jerk my chin in the direction I mean.

She follows with her gaze and nods.

"Just through that gap, there's a boat moored. We take that back."

She frowns, a tiny divot appearing between her eyes.

"What?" I ask her.

"Did you use the boat to get here before me? That feels an awful lot like cheating."

I shake my head. "We didn't. I swear to you. It was moored here days before the games started."

"An awful lot of planning seems to go into this."

"Of course there is," Rafferty states with some pride. "It takes planning to make sure things run smoothly. We might have unusual tastes, but that doesn't mean we're idiots. When we aren't doing this, we run a highly professional operation on this island."

"Didn't mean to cause offense," she mutters.

Another huge yawn from her has me realizing she'll be asleep the moment we get her back to the villa.

When we reach the boat, I clamber in first and take a seat with her still in my arms. Rafferty grabs a blanket from the seat opposite and covers her with it. She sighs and snuggles in, and there goes that twinge in my heart again.

Once we set off, bouncing over the smooth ocean on the way back the compound, Honor's breathing settles into an even rhythm. She's asleep with her head on my shoulder and her warm, naked skin filling my arms. I could get used to this.

"You look comfortable," Asher says, an edge to his tone.

I ignore him.

"She's a paid bit of fun, Wilder. Nothing more."

I grit my jaw and still don't respond.

"Just don't get too into her." He shakes his head. "She'll be gone in a few days."

"Anyway, it's not what we do," Brody adds. "We have a purpose, and this is just rest and relaxation."

I sigh and shut them out for a while. The guys are okay, we get along, and we have a bond because of the one man we're all trying to get our revenge on, but if I had to choose them as friends, I'd realistically probably only have something in common with Brody.

When we reach the compound, I step off the boat and carry a still sleeping Honor into the building.

"We fucked her unconscious." Asher sneers.

I'm itching to fucking punch him in the mouth, and that's not normal. He's right. I need to tone this down. Can't go catching feelings for her.

"I'm taking her to her room," I say to no one in particular and march down the hallway.

Once in her room, I pull the covers back and place her carefully in bed. She sighs and hugs her pillow, and still doesn't wake. I consider covering her naked form with the sheets but change my mind. She looks too good to cover up. Thinking she's going to be dehydrated when she awakes, I head into the kitchen and pour her some water. Then I take it to her, place the glass on the side, and watch her.

I stay there like a creeper for a good five minutes, watching Honor sleep. Fuck, she really is beautiful. Her dark lashes rest upon her creamy cheeks, and her pink lips are parted slightly. Her eyes dart beneath her eyelids, telling me she's fully asleep now.

I should probably leave, but I can't bring myself to do it. My palms burn with the desire to touch that perfect, pale skin. I move around to the other side of the bed and carefully climb onto the bed behind her. I'm conscious of my size and the way the bed dips with my weight. Will it be enough to wake her?

Pausing, I wait to see if she stirs. Honor exhales lightly but doesn't move.

Blood rushes to my cock. She's so vulnerable right now, and that turns me on. The others like to rib me about my fetish for small and delicate women, but I like what I like.

Right now, I'd like nothing more than to free myself from my pants and push myself between her sweet thighs, but I

BLURRED LIMITS

know I can't. My dick isn't something you can just spring on someone.

I lean in closer and inhale the sweet perfume of her hair. I can't deny the fact she also absolutely stinks of sex. The mingling of all of our cum, combined with her own juices, and that of the sun lotion she'd used is intoxicating. I wish I could bottle it and use it whenever I need to jack off.

I risk moving closer, so I can press my erection against the small of her back, right above her bare ass. Not wanting to wake her, I don't dare apply too much pressure, but just the brush of contact between us is enough to make my balls tighten with pleasure. I lean in and place the flat of my tongue against her bare shoulder and lick her skin. She tastes of salt and something undeniably her.

Fuck. It's all I can do not to free myself and masturbate over her. Maybe if this was a different girl, I would have, but I can't bring myself to defile her while she's sleeping. I'm not completely restrained, however. I want to get a feel of her, so I can take the memory back to my room and hold it in my mind while I work my cock.

She's wrapped around the pillow, so as much as I'd like to get a handful of those gorgeous tits, I can't. Instead, I focus on the one part of her exposed to me—her ass. I lightly brush my palm over the sweet curve of her cheek. It's firm and smooth and peachy, the skin still pink from where she'd been spanked. I dip my finger between the cleft and slowly run it down, over her tight asshole. She murmurs and wriggles slightly. I freeze, but then she settles, so I keep going. I move lower and slip between her folds. She's still wet, and I dip my fingertip in her juices. I'd love to fingerfuck her right now, and it takes all my restraint not to push my digits inside her pussy and work her until she comes, but I don't want to risk her using the safeword and quitting before tomorrow.

With my cock straining painfully against the front of my pants, I carefully maneuver myself back off the bed. It's taken every ounce of self-restraint not to do exactly what I want to her, but I tell myself it'll be worth the wait.

Then I do something I don't even understand myself. I lean in, kiss her gently on the forehead, and whisper, "Sweet dreams, Snow."

Leaving, I close the door softly behind me and go find the guys, who I presume will be in the den.

They are, but when I join them, there's a look of fury on Rafferty's face.

"What's up?"

Rafferty turns to me. "Two things. One is the PI we have looking into Pastor Wren has some news."

My stomach lurches. Just hearing the name has me back there. I was small then. A runt of a kid. He was the church pastor. Our church wasn't small, it was huge, and Wren was a powerful and wealthy man. He abused his position in ways no man ever should, and it went on for years as he traveled around the country with his church.

Both the traveling and the difference of age between the four of us was the reason none of us had met back then. He'd already moved on from me when Rafferty met him, and Rafferty was out of his life before Brody showed up. Asher was the last one of us to gain Pastor Wren's attention. Wren only liked us at a certain age, and so when we got too old for him, he moved on to the next. There are eleven years between me and Asher. That the abuse spanned that amount of time, at a minimum, makes me sick.

I push the memory aside before it makes me panic or rage in a way that means damage to this room I'm standing in.

"And?"

"He thinks he might have a lead on his whereabouts. Looks like he changed his name, but he's still preaching." Rafferty rakes a hand through his normally neat hair, making it stick out. "Which means he has access to young kids."

"Fucking fucker," Asher spits out. "This means we might finally have a chance to catch up with him."

"Where is he?" I ask.

"If it is him, and we're awaiting definite confirmation on it, then he's not too far. Preaching in a mega church in Reno."

Fucking piece of shit. I want to go there right now and tear his head from his body. I won't, though, because this we do together. It's the deal.

"You said two things?"

"Yeah." Brody looks pissed. Really pissed. "I knew there was something off about her," he snarls. "Our Pandora."

Honor. *Shit*.

"What is it?" I demand of Rafferty.

"Asher was just speed running through the security tapes like we do, and he saw Honor leave her room last night."

"So?" I shrug. "She's not a prisoner."

"She went snooping. Ended up in the staffroom, got into her locker and messed about with her phone." Rafferty blows out a breath. "I told her, it's clear as day in the contract, too. No phones while she's here."

"Did she call someone?" I ask.

"Nope," Asher says, joining in the convo. "She looked at it, turned it off, shoved it back in her bag, and went back to bed."

Oh, for fuck's sake. These guys. "Listen. You're all on edge because we finally have a lead on Wren. So what? She checked her phone."

"She broke the rules," Rafferty states.

"And? Jesus. She checked her phone then turned it off. Maybe she wanted some battery left for when she gets out of here. You ever think of that?"

Rafferty raises his brows. "Yeah, no. That could be it, I suppose."

"Something's not right, I'm telling you." Brody starts pacing.

"For now, can we focus on one thing and decide what to do about the pastor?" I ask them.

Asher laughs, but it's bitter as black coffee. "You're into her. That's not what this should be about."

"I'm not into her." It's a lie, and I can taste it as soon as I say it. *Liar, liar, fucking pants on fire.*

"I say we watch her a little more closely tomorrow," Rafferty says. "Wilder makes a good point, but Brody seems convinced something is off with her, so we watch her, and we see."

Chapter Eighteen
Honor

I WAKE TO FIND MYSELF back in bed.

It's dark, so still evening.

The memory of getting here comes back to me in tiny glimpses. Strong arms, a broad chest, the swell and ebb of the ocean beneath us. Then the bedroom, and—unless I'd dreamed it—forehead kisses.

The sheets are scratchy with sand. My body aches, especially between my thighs. I have what I assume is a 'just fucked' hangover. The skin on my ass and thighs is still sensitive and tender from the spanking I'd received.

Those bastards.

How am I going to last three more games? We've only reached the second one, and I already feel like I've taken way more than I can handle.

I remember how Brody talked about taking my ass. Had he been serious? God, taking Rafferty's cock inside my pussy had been painful enough. How can I possibly fit a dick inside that particular hole? The idea is terrifying, but what choice will I have if that's what they decide to do?

I can leave. I can use the safeword and get the hell out of here.

Then I'll be vulnerable to *him* finding me again.

I find myself weighing up which is the lesser of two evils—these men on the island who want to use me for sex, or the man on the mainland who I don't doubt wants me dead.

At least these four men make no secret about who they are and what they want. They might be fucked up in their sexual tastes—wanting to hunt a woman across the island only to pass her between them—but they make sure we're taken care of and that we know what we're getting into. We've got an out if it all gets too much. They've put the choice in my hands.

A tall glass of water sits on the nightstand. Who poured that for me? Had it been Wilder? For a man who looks so big and scary, I'm starting to wonder if he has a soft side. Then I remember his monster cock shoving between my lips, the way the piercing caught against the soft palate of my mouth, the way he'd come over my tongue and then my mouth. He'd used me like I was an inanimate object.

I cover my face with my hands. "Oh, God."

What have I done? I'm not sure I even recognize myself anymore. I've always considered myself to be a good person, but how can I possibly think that now? I let four men I don't even like use me in the worst possible way. Even worse, there was a part of me that enjoyed it.

A flutter goes through my core as I think about it. The way Brody's tongue had worked my pussy had been insane. I'd never had a man lick me in such a way. He hadn't just done a few flicks to my clit—he'd penetrated me with his entire tongue, fucking me with it like he would with a cock.

I'd sucked off two different men and swallowed two different lots of cum. Who did that? No respectable woman, that was for sure. And Wilder's dick...holy hell. I squeezed my thighs together as another wave of excitement rolled through me. I hated myself for thinking about it in any way other than horror. I was sure I'd read somewhere that certain piercings were done to hit a woman's G-spot. Had he had it done in order to give a woman more pleasure? That someone could put themselves through something like that to pleasure another person seemed insane.

It was so big, and that piercing as well...would it rip me up inside, or would it feel incredible?

I have the feeling that if I last the next few days, I'm going to find out.

There had been a moment of gentleness with Rafferty. I don't know if he'd believed me about me being a virgin, but he'd taken things slowly—at least he had after the cuffs and spanking. I'd never had an orgasm like that in my life. I didn't even know they could feel so intense.

I should hate this place, should be desperate to leave, but the truth is that it feels like a bit of a sanctuary. I've lived so long in such dire circumstances, often with no real bed or roof over my head, constantly feeling as though I'm going to be attacked or robbed, or both, that this is a little piece of luxury. I've been constantly on high alert, not only fearful of random strangers, but also that the man I've run from would catch up with me. It's very hard to say no to such a place when you've experienced what I have. Only a matter of days ago, the offer of a couch to sleep on would have felt like bliss.

That I'm no longer alone is also a comfort. I might only be keeping my current company because they want to use me, but I also get the feeling that if anyone tried to fuck with what was theirs, they'd come down on them like an atomic bomb. I try to picture my stepfather's face if he had to stand up to Wilder and the others. Don is not a man who's easily intimidated, but these men are something else.

Their protection won't last for long. In a few days, I'll be leaving this place, and them. I don't know if I should feel relieved or disappointed at the thought.

A knock comes at my door, and I pull the sheets around my naked body, worried someone will burst in. No one does, so, with the sheet wrapped around me, I open the door to find a tray of food—cold hams, bread, olives, balsamic vinegar, and olive oil—waiting for me. It's simple fare, but I'm ravenous after all the exercise of the day.

I carry it back to the bed and demolish it all in one go. I've not been brought any wine tonight—I suppose that would have been my reward if I'd won.

I guess that means I won't be invited for dinner tonight. I've been secretly hoping the guys might come by to see me. I check myself. This is sex, that's all. A contract. I can't go kidding myself that any of them think anything more of me than that. I'm nothing special. They've done exactly this with God-knows how many women before me.

I don't feel anything for them either, I remind myself. I'm in this for the money. I've lied to them for the money. I know nothing about them, and they know even less about me. They don't even know my real name.

I wish I could shrug off the sense of shame that's settled in the pit of my stomach. I should just own this—accept what I've lowered myself to and figure out how to deal with it. There's no one else I can blame—not even the men. No one forced me to put myself in this position. I did it to myself the minute I kept my mouth shut when I realized they thought I was someone else. I've had the power within me to stop it at any time, and I kept my lips firmly shut—or at least I did when I wasn't sucking dick.

Slut.
Whore.
Bitch.
Liar.

So many derogatory words—words I'd never use against another woman or would expect someone else to say about me—go through my head. No one can say or think anything worse than I think about myself. I have no problem with anyone who wants to be promiscuous, as long as they're consenting and safe, but it's never been how I think about myself.

I won't be using my vibrator tonight, that's for sure. I'm far too sore to be thinking about that.

I select a clean silky nightdress and a pair of panties, and set them out together with a thick fluffy towel. If I'm not going to have the company of the men tonight, I'll treat myself to a long soak in the tub, and then I'll get an early night.

Chapter Nineteen
Asher

I'M UP EARLY, EAGER to get the day started.

Yesterday, all I got from Honor was a hand on my cock. Brody got to eat out her sweet little pussy, both Rafferty and Wilder had her suck their dicks, and then Rafferty fucked her virgin cunt.

I definitely don't feel as though I've really had my time with Honor yet. That's okay. I understand why. I can get a little...carried away...when I'm caught up in the moment. It's like I get tunnel vision and I struggle to break out of it. That's why I need the others around me. They're always here to step in when it looks like I've lost control. I can be dangerous, and I'm fully aware of that.

I don't trust myself either.

It's day three now, and while she'll be well rested, she'll also be sore and aching, both from the distance across the island she's been covering each day and from the sex. The longer this goes on, the easier it is to catch them. And the easier it is to catch them, the further we push them, physically, mentally, and sexually.

No woman has made it to the end yet without using the safeword and tapping out. I chuckle as I remember one of them held down by me and Rafferty while she tried to take both Brody's and Wilder's cocks in her pussy at the same time. We'd lubed her up plenty, and I'd practically fisted her before that to make sure she'd been good and stretched, but the minute she tried sinking down on both cocks, she'd turned white and bailed.

Can't say I blamed her.

My laptop pings with a message, and I hit a key to bring it to life.

I frown.

One message received: *FunnelWeb01*

Honor's online name.

What the hell? How can Honor be sending me a message when she has no access to tech in our home?

Her username is that of a spider. It's common enough—we're on the dark web, after all, and the mention of webs brings spiders to mind. But now I've actually met Honor, I struggle to align her with the name she'd chosen for her online self. In fact, there's a lot that doesn't quite fit. When she'd flirted with us online, she'd come across as confident and sure of herself. She'd been pretty graphic when she'd explained exactly what she wanted us to do to her—how she wanted to be chased and caught and held down while we took whatever we wanted from her over and over. That was why we'd thought it was such a good match. The money would have just been a bonus to her, a way of getting her to stay once she realized exactly how much we did take. We find it also helps up the stakes on both sides of the game. As much as this is roleplay, we want the game to be real.

I push my glasses up my nose. How is she messaging us? I remember she'd gone to find her phone last night. Is she playing with us?

A strange sensation creeps into my stomach. I don't like it. It's unease. Something feels wrong, and all my internal warning systems are blaring. My skin prickles all over.

I click to open the message.

Please forgive me. I'm so sorry I've missed our game. I've been in an accident and only just had access to the internet and been well enough to get in touch. I hope you're not too mad at me.

What the fuck is this? My mind spins. Is this some kind of game—a way for Honor to get back at us? But why would she say she's not here when she is? Furthermore, this cannot be from Honor because how is she messaging me without a phone, or access to any tech?

I shove back my chair. "Motherfucker."

There are only two explanations, and I don't like either of them. Either Honor sent the message last night after sneaking about, and she's trying to play some kind of fucked-up game with us, or else the woman we've been chasing across the island, and fucking, isn't the same one we'd been talking to online.

I need to speak to the others. They're not going to like this. Brody had kept saying that something was up with her, and I have a sinking sensation he might have been right.

If Honor isn't the woman we've been talking to online, who the hell is she?

My stomach is a knot as I scoop up my laptop. I'll find Rafferty first. He's the one who funds this whole thing, so he has the most to lose if we've fucked up somewhere along the line. He's also the one who tends to be ruled more by his head than his heart, unlike Wilder and Brody, who can both let their tempers and other emotions get the best of them.

To my surprise, I find all three of them already in the office. I clearly wasn't the only one keen to get the day started. Unfortunately, I suspect the news I'm about to deliver is going to throw a curveball at things.

"We've got a problem," I announce.

Rafferty's brow pinches. "What's happened?"

I shove my laptop under his nose. "We received a message."

"So?"

"Look who it's from."

Brody and Wilder have risen from where they were sitting to join me and Rafferty. They stand behind us so they can get a view of the screen.

"FunnelWeb01," Rafferty reads. "Honor. Why has she messaged us?"

"To apologize for not coming," I say.

His head snaps around at me. "What?"

Wilder straightens. "That doesn't make sense."

"Did she send it last night when she went to get her phone?" Rafferty suggests. "Some sort of mindfuck?"

"That's what I thought, but look at the time of the message." I stab my finger at the screen.

Brody leans in to read it. "Six a.m. this morning."

I nod. "Nowhere near the time she used her phone."

"Could she have set the message to send at a later date?" Wilder says.

I twist to face him. "And why the fuck would she do that?"

He shrugs his massive shoulders. "Maybe she's trying to mess with us."

"Does she really seem the type?" It's been obvious that Wilder has a soft spot for our little plaything, but I don't want that to muddy his judgement.

Brody drags his hand through his scruffy blond hair. "Fuuuuck. I always knew there was something up with her." He slams his palm against the back of the chair. "I should have trusted my goddamned instinct."

"Wait a minute." Rafferty holds up one hand. "What are we saying here?"

I arch both eyebrows. "That the most obvious explanation is normally the right one."

"We could reply to the message," Brody says, jerking his chin at the laptop. "Honor is in her room right now. If we get a reply, we know it wasn't her."

I nod. "Good idea." My fingers fly across the keyboard, typing out a reply. *We're sorry to hear that. You have been missed. Let us know if you want to reschedule.* I sign it off as the resort name. *The Limit.*

Dots appear on screen, and I glance to the others. "She's online."

Brody goes to our security cameras. He flicks through the screens until he brings up the one of Honor's room. Sure enough, she's curled up on her side on the bed, her hand tucked in under her cheek. A spurt of anger roils through me. She looks so peaceful and innocent, but that's not who she is at all. She's a fucking liar, and she's been playing us this whole time.

A reply pops up on screen. *Yes, please. I'm so disappointed I'm not there. I'll let you know as soon as I'm well enough.*

I slam down the laptop lid. "Fuck."

All our eyes are drawn back to the image of the girl asleep in bed. Her dark hair is spread out across the pillow like a halo. Her legs are bare against the white of the sheets. The cream silk nightdress she's wearing hugs every curve so perfectly she might as well be naked. If she's not the woman we'd arranged to come to the island for our game, who the fuck is she?

Brody rubs his hand over his mouth. "We should have been more careful."

"How?" Rafferty asks. "How could we have ever predicted this happening? What crazy person would put themselves forward to take part in our games in the place of someone else?"

My brain is turning everything over. I speak slowly, as I'm putting together what's happened. "The trouble is, we've been *too* careful. Even though we use the dark net to find our 'toys,' we're still careful never to use real names or even our faces. We get glimpses of the girls we bring here—a photograph of parts of their bodies, their faces hidden. We see enough to know they're someone we'd be attracted to, but not enough that we'd recognize them in the street. It's not until they come to the island that we ensure we have names and signatures."

"Shit," Wilder says, "Asher is right. How would we ever know she was someone else? We just assumed."

Something else occurs to me. "Do you think she used her real name?"

Rafferty narrows his eyes at me. "Why?"

"If she didn't, and she's just been making shit up, then that contract she signed is worthless."

Anger flashes across Rafferty's face. "We've been playing this game with a contract that's null and void?"

I nod. "If she's used a fake name, then yeah."

Rafferty has paled. "She could leave this place and announce to the world exactly what we do here. What if she's a journalist or something? Remember that time a journalist wanted to do the ordinary survival, evasion, and capture shit we do, and we said no? What if this is like that?"

"We must have seen papers," Brody says. "Felicity went through the paperwork with her. Felicity knows what she's doing."

"Was the mistake at her level, then?" I say. "Why would she think Honor was our girl when she wasn't?"

Rafferty shakes his head. "Felicity only dealt with the one person our pilot, Phelps, brought over to the island. If a mistake was made, then it starts with him."

We're going to need to talk to everyone involved, but the first person I want to talk to is Honor.

Wilder folds his arms across his chest. "We should go and ask Honor straight."

"Why the fuck should we be straight with her when she hasn't been with us?" I snort. "She's played with us. We don't know who or what the fuck she is. I won't be letting her get away with this so easily."

There's no point in wasting any more time. I head for the door without bothering to check that the others are coming with me. I know they will.

The four of us storm through the hotel, toward Honor's room. Rage radiates off us all. We're not people who like to be tricked. Brody would be furious with himself for not trusting his instincts. Wilder will be kicking himself for developing feelings for her. Rafferty will be going all mama-bear over the possibility that her lies have put *The Limit* in jeopardy.

With me leading the way, we burst into her room.

She shoots upright at the intrusion and clambers from the bed. She's grabbed a pillow as she does so, and clutches it to her body, as though it'll offer her some kind of protection. She's going to need a lot more than a fucking pillow. It's clear she's realized something is wrong, her gaze darting between us.

"What—what's happening?"

I don't waste any time. "What's your username, Honor?"

The color drains from her face. "What?"

"Online. When we were talking before you came here. What username have you been using?"

"Why do you need to know that?"

"I couldn't remember it, and I wanted to go over our old messages."

She blinks twice in quick succession. "I—I can't remember it either."

I frown and purse my lips. "Really? You can't remember your own username?"

"I have a terrible memory."

I pretend to think for a moment. "It was something to do with birds, wasn't it? Bird of Paradise."

Relief flashes across her delicate features. "Yes, that was it. I'm sure you'll be able to find me with that info."

I'm done playing games. "Don't fucking lie to me."

"What?"

"Your username had nothing to do with birds."

"Oh, of—"

I don't give her a chance to finish her sentence. I've heard enough. I spring forward and wrap my hand around her throat, shoving her up against the wall. She drops the pillow, and it falls at my feet.

"Don't fucking lie to me!"

Her blue eyes widen with shock, her pretty, pink lips parting. I squeeze tighter, and she gives a strange, strangled squeak that sends blood rushing to my cock. Her skin is warm and soft, so pliable. Her pulse quickens against my fingertips.

"Who the fuck are you?"

I squeeze harder, and she batters her fists against my forearms and shoulders. I feel cold satisfaction. This is what I like, having this power over women. I like to watch the fear in their eyes, ideally when I have their cunts wrapped around my cock.

"Asher," Wilder's warning tone comes from over my shoulder, "that's enough."

I release her throat, but this won't be the end.

Chapter Twenty
Honor

I DROP TO MY KNEES on the floor, my hands automatically going to my throat. I cough as air rushes down my bruised windpipe and fills my lungs. For a moment, I'd been terrified Asher would kill me.

I'm relieved when his white sneakers are replaced by Rafferty's dress shoes, but the relief only lasts for a moment.

Fingers yank my chin up, gripping hard. Rafferty forces me to meet his eye—blue on blue. "Is Honor even your real name?"

My blood turns to ice.

Oh, God. They know.

I was an idiot thinking I was going to get away with this. Of course they were going to find out eventually.

Tears prick the corners of my eyes. I nod—a tiny movement, as he still holds my chin tight. "Yes, it is." My voice is hoarse.

"Honor Harper?" he clarifies.

There's no point in continuing with the lie. "No, not my surname."

"Then who the fuck are you? How did you get onto the island?"

"My name's Honor Armitage. I—I was supposed to be starting a job as a maid. I got here early because I didn't have anywhere else to go. I didn't know that I'd be mistaken for someone else."

I tremble under their scrutiny, sensing myself shrinking, wanting to vanish.

"The maid?" he says in disbelief. "You're supposed to be the *fucking maid*?"

"I'm sorry. I didn't mean to lie to you, but Felicity told me about the money, and I was desperate."

Brody snorts in derision. "We've been screwing the maid."

Rafferty releases my chin and snaps around at him. "This isn't fucking funny, Brody."

"Yeah, I know that, dude. Believe me, I know. I tried to tell you all something was off with her, and no one listened."

I don't want them to turn on each other, but I'd rather they were arguing together than all staring at me.

Does this mean the two hundred grand won't be mine? I want to ask the question, but I don't want to make them even angrier.

"Do—do you want me to leave?"

Asher takes a step froward. "Leave? Why would we want you to do that?"

I rear back, terrified he'll try to strangle me again. "Because...umm...I'm here under false pretenses."

"You think we're just going to let you waltz out of here?" Rafferty says. "We're extremely careful to ensure no one comes here who isn't protected by a contract, and you signed that contract, but in a fake name. That makes the contract worthless. You could leave the island and tell whoever you wanted about this place with no fear of reprisal."

"I won't," I tell him. "I swear it."

Brody scoffs. "You think we're going to believe you? After you've done nothing but lie to us for days?"

"I can sign a new contract in my real name," I blurt. "I'll sign whatever you want."

I realize this will leave a paper trail my stepfather might be able to follow. The thought churns my stomach. No, these guys have all their online security well protected, don't they? Don Bowen has a lot of contacts in high places, but what are the chances of him ever cracking this place? It seems pretty low to me, but not impossible. Never impossible. After all, aren't I living proof that these men are capable of making mistakes?

What choice do I have? I leave here, today, without a cent to my name and with nowhere to go. I want to cry at the sheer desperation of my situation. A darkness swirls inside me, tempting me, luring me in. What is even the point in carrying on?

No, I pull myself out of it with a sharp mental tug. I'm stronger than that. I won't just give in. My stepfather is still out there, and even if I'm dead, there's nothing to stop him destroying a whole other innocent family. He'll lure some other single mother into his lair with his nice smile and good clothes and respectable job, and then dismantle everything that makes them happy, piece by piece.

"Let me continue the game," I beg. "I'll sign a new contract. We can even start over, if you want. Start from game one, so it's fair."

What the hell am I doing to myself? Giving them more chances to catch me and use me and humiliate me. A horrible sneaking suspicion slips through me. Is there a part of me that's actually enjoyed this? Yes, it's a means to an end, but do I like the thought of them chasing me across the island and using me in that way? It allows me to keep up the act that I'm a good girl—if only to myself—by fighting them and making out that I don't want it, while also giving in to my darkest fantasies. I can't pretend I haven't imagined how it'll feel to have Wilder's huge, pierced cock stretch me open while the others pin me down or worse.

"It's too late for that," Brody snaps.

I hate that they're so angry with me. That had never been my intention. My fears around being found out had always mainly centered around not getting the money, but to my surprise, I discover that I'm hurt that they're thinking badly of me.

The tears that have been filling my eyes slide down my cheeks. "So, you're going to make me leave? I—I don't have anywhere to go, and there's this man—"

Rafferty cuts his gaze back to mine. "A man? A boyfriend? An ex?"

Have I wrongfooted myself again by mentioning this? "He's my stepfather."

His eyes narrow, his forehead pinching. "So?"

"I just don't want him to find me."

"And you thought if you came here, we'd what, exactly? Protect you?"

"I didn't mean to lie to you. I *did* have a reason to come here. Your housekeeper employed me as a maid. I have a real job here. I didn't come onto the island under false pretenses. Then Felicity thought I was someone else, and the others did, too, and I just went along with it."

"You mean you were never into what we were doing?" He rubs his hand across his mouth. "Jesus Fucking Christ. I fucked you, and you *were* a virgin. A virgin fucking maid. We did all those things to you..." He shakes his head and turns away from me as though he can't even bear to look at me anymore.

I can sense the others all staring at me, and I've never felt so small in my life. Images of them standing over me, of me sucking cock and spreading my legs, and taking their cum in my face fills me with utter shame. These men thought I was doing those things because I enjoyed it, because I'd come here to fulfill a kink, but I'd revealed myself as a liar, and not only that, a greedy liar.

Wilder snarls. "She was just in it for the fucking money."

I can't even deny it. "I'm sorry."

"Not good enough," he growls.

Any tenderness I've seen in him has completely vanished.

On shaking legs, and using the wall behind me as support, I push myself to standing. "It's okay. I'll leave. Forget I ever existed."

"Uh-uh, not so fast, Pandora."

Brody has blocked my way.

Fear spikes through me. What's he doing?

He continues. "I say we're in this for real now."

Wait a minute. What's he saying? "I—I don't understand."

He glances over his shoulder to get the approval of the others. "No contract, no safeword. We own you now."

I shake my head. "No, please." This sounds dangerous.

I mentally run through possible plans. There's no way I can swim to the mainland, but there are several small boats left in coves around the island. I've already been in two of them. I have no idea how to drive a boat, but I'd definitely give it a go, if needed.

But if I run, there'll be no chance of getting the money. I feel like I've already done the hard part—I'm no longer a virgin. Surely, I deserve something for this.

It seems no matter which choice I make, I'm not going to win.

Asher moves closer, a sneer across his face. "Sweet little Honor. You're ours now. We tried to do everything right, and you fucked us over. You took us for fools. You think we're just going to let you get away with that?"

The magnitude of what I've done swells around me.

I'd thought these men were a lesser evil, but now I wonder.

Despite hating myself for asking this question, I have to know. "And will I get my money at the end of it?"

"Fucking bitch," Wilder snarls, raking his hand through his long hair. "It's still all about the money, isn't it? You act so sweet and innocent, but you're not better than a woman who stands on a street corner at night. You're willing to hand yourself over to us just as long as you get paid."

He's right, of course.

He shoots me a glare that's almost animalistic. "And to think I'd almost allowed myself to like you, Snow."

I almost wilt at his words, but now isn't the time to soften. The only thing I've got left is to play it hard. "If you're not going to let me leave and I have to put up with you four degenerates, the least I should get is what is owed to me."

Rafferty folds his arms across his chest, his handsome face schooled into an impassive mask. "We don't owe you anything. We owed *FunnelWeb01* both the money and a good time, and you stole that from her. It's how this place works—all consenting adults, no matter how depraved or violent things might get. Everyone is on the same page. You took that from us. We thought you were someone else, and we fucked you like it was what you wanted. How do you think that makes us look?"

"I'm sorry," I say again. "I'm sorry, I'm sorry, I'm sorry."

"The damage is already done," Asher says with a smirk. "Why stop now?"

I've already suggested to them that we continue with a new contract. There's no point in me repeating myself. I don't think it'll matter what I say now. These men will decide between them what happens to me next. I have no choice but to go along with their decision.

"How about we make a deal?" Rafferty says. "But you have to show us how much you want it."

My stomach flutters with anxiety. "What kind of a deal?"

"We restart the game, only this time it's for real. No more safeword. No comfortable beds and seafood platters. You run from us, we find you, and we fuck you. You agree to this, and you're ours."

I hate to ask, but I have to. "And the money?"

"It'll be yours after five days, if you can handle five days."

"Are you going to give me much of a choice?"

"Yes. We can fuck you, and you don't get the money."

I bark out a cold laugh. "That doesn't seem like much of a choice to me."

"You didn't give us much of a choice when you pretended to be someone else."

He has a point. His words sting.

"Or you can just leave," he continues. "I'm still going to make you sign a contract in your real name to ensure you don't ever speak of this place or what happens here, but then you leave without a cent. We won't lay another finger on you, however much you don't deserve to get off scot-free. We'll just dump you back on the mainland and leave you, like the trash you are."

They're giving me a lifeline. It's a tenuous one, and I'm not sure I even deserve it. I'm probably making a huge mistake by even considering it. I won't have an out any longer. They'll be able to do whatever they want to me, and it won't matter how much I want them to stop, I won't be able to make them.

I've brought this upon myself.

The money.

Five days.

Freedom.

It's just sex, I tell myself. I've already done the hard part—losing my virginity. I just have to open my legs and my mouth and shut my eyes and let them get on with it. After five days, I can take their cash and forget any of this ever happened. I don't want to be that girl, but I also don't want to be the girl living on the streets with nothing where I'll probably end up attacked at some point anyway. This will set me up for my whole future.

And there's the little dark part of me that freakishly likes the idea. That messed up, deep, hidden part of me I don't want to examine to closely because she freaks me out. I should be terrified. I *am* terrified, but there's also this tiny ripple of excitement that simply shouldn't be there.

I swallow. "Okay. I'll do it."

Rafferty studies my face, then he steps forward and boxes me in with his arms, with both his hands on the wall either side of my head.

"Today doesn't count. Got it? Today is just to make sure you're in this fully."

"I am."

"Let's see how much of a whore you are."

He releases one hand from the wall and pushes it beneath the flimsy hem of my nightdress. My miniscule panties are barely more than a piece of string, but he wraps his fingers around the side of them and tears them from my body. The material cuts into my skin, and I yelp. I have no doubt they'll have left a mark.

Roughly, he shoves two fingers inside me, deep into my core. It hurts, especially with me still being so sore from the previous day. My inner walls are bruised, and my clit still swollen. Tears blur my vision then slip down my cheeks, and with his other hand, he thumbs them away.

He turns to look at the others. "She's wet. Always so wet and ready."

He crooks his fingers inside me, brushing the sweet spot on my inner wall. I gasp and then groan, and my hips—those traitorous things—push forward. His thumb sweeps over my clit, and it's like an instant electric shock, melting my core. My nipples pebble beneath my nightdress, the points obvious under the barely-there material.

"You might be a liar," he says, "but you're a horny fucking liar."

He pumps his fingers in and out of me a couple more times, building me higher. My stomach and thigh muscles are rigid with tension, and it's all I can do not to drop my head to his chest and clutch my fingers into his muscular shoulders. But I don't touch him, instead remaining up against the wall, with my hands clenched into fists at my side.

He continues to finger fuck me, and my breathing grows coarse. A whimper escapes me. "Oh, fuck. Oh, God." I'm close...so close.

Suddenly, he pulls his fingers from my body, and it's like he's pulled the plug out of me.

He leans in close and speaks in my ear. "Go on then, bitch. *Run.*"

I suck in a breath and realize what's expected from me.

I dart between them, and they let me go. In seconds, I'm out of the room and running down the corridor. I'm barefooted and only in the tiny silky nightdress I'd slept in. I don't even have any underwear on now, and I'm slippery between my thighs. There's no point in me running outside. The rocky terrain of the island will cut my feet to pieces, and my outfit offers me no shelter from the sun or biting insects.

I stay in the hotel, my feet thumping across the plush carpet. Which way should I go? Heading up will only take me to *their* domain, so I find the stairwell and run down. I don't want to go to the staff quarters. I think of bumping into Felicity and her asking what this is all about. I can't stand the thought of another person looking at me with such disgust.

The men aren't far behind me. They didn't give me much of a head start this time. I shouldn't be surprised. No rules anymore, remember? They can do whatever they want.

I run down corridors and push through doors, until I find myself in what must be the spa. There's a small plunge pool with wooden sun loungers around it, complete with white waterproof mattresses and equally white towels. Lush greenery stands in pots in each corner, but I realize it must be fake since there's no natural sunlight in here to keep the plants alive. The place is deserted.

I look left and right. Fuck. There's no way out of here other than the way I came. No, that can't be right. There must be a fire exit somewhere.

The men pour through the door after me, and I spin to face them. It's too late to find an exit now.

"Please," I beg, though I'm not even sure what it is I'm begging for. Them to be gentle with me, I suppose. I don't think that's going to happen.

Brody stalks over to me and in one swift move tears the nightdress from my body. I'm left completely naked, and I do my best to hide my nudity with my hands. It's a futile act. They'll see right into me—literally making me spread my legs for them—if that's what they want.

"Get on the lounger," Rafferty commands. "On all fours."

There's no point in refusing. We've come to an agreement. I've sold my soul—and body—to these men.

Choking back tears, I do as he says. The sun lounger mattress is thick and spongy, and my knees and palms sink into it. I feel so exposed like this. I stare down at the white foam, and a tear runs off the end of my nose and drips down, forming a dark circle on the material.

"Get condoms and lube," Rafferty tells one of the others. "There'll be some in the storeroom."

I don't look up to see which one goes to get it.

A moment later, Brody's deep voice sounds out. "Got it. Does this mean what I think it does."

"I took her virgin pussy yesterday. Now one of you can take her virgin ass."

I tense. Oh, God.

"Go on, Asher," Rafferty says. "Your turn."

This is the man who has left bruises around my throat and who I thought, not long ago, was going to kill me. Now he's going to fuck me in the ass, and I have no doubt that he won't be gentle.

Asher takes off his black framed glasses and slips them into the top pocket of his shirt. "Wouldn't want to steam them up."

I bite my lower lip and keep my mouth shut.

Asher kneels behind me. "Such a pretty ass," he croons. His hot palms land on my bottom, spreading my ass cheeks.

"What are you doing?" I gasp.

"What does it look like?"

"No, please." Panic bubbles through me. I try to move, but his strong hand on my lower back holds me in place.

His finger prods at my back hole and then pushes inside with a burn. Oh, fuck. This isn't good.

"You want to play our game, baby girl?" Asher says from over my shoulder. "Tell us how much you want it, or you can walk."

I swallow hard. Want it? Want what, exactly? For him to take me *that* way? I should already know that this is the sort of thing I'm letting myself in for if I continue. It's not just about the money. It's also about safety. If I leave with nothing, I'm back out on the streets.

It occurs to me that they're taking advantage of a vulnerable girl, but then wasn't I the one to take advantage of them first?

"I—"

He silences me with a second finger, stretching me. At least he's used lube, but it still hurts. Oh, fuck. It burns. I turn my face to one side and bite the inside of my bicep to prevent myself crying out.

"Hurts, doesn't it, princess? You wait until it's a cock."

"No, please."

"We like it when women beg. Even better when they fight back."

But I can't fight back. I have to do this.

His fingers are deep inside me, filling me, working my body. I can feel myself getting wet, my skin prickling with an arousal I don't even want, my head growing foggy.

"That's good," Asher said. "Loosening up nicely. I think you're ready for more."

I still don't lift my head, but I hear the click of a belt buckle followed by the rasp of his zipper.

The smooth head presses against my hole, and my whole body goes rigid. I've agreed to this. What the fuck was I thinking?

"You need to relax, or this is going to hurt a whole lot more than it needs to."

I can hear the amusement in Asher's tone. The fucker wants it to hurt.

In desperation, the safeword bursts from my lips. "Ragnarök," I cry. "Ragnarök, Ragnarök!"

"That word was in the contract," he snarls. "The contract you signed under a fake name, remember? It doesn't mean a fucking thing."

He's right. The fucker.

"Someone take care of her clit," he says.

Wilder steps in. "Let me."

He maneuvers himself between me and the sun lounger, wriggling down to bring his face level with my pussy. The position means Asher has to straddle Wilder's torso, too, but neither of the men seem to mind.

Now, I'm no longer on all fours on the bed, but higher up so my hands are now braced on the back of the lounger. Wilder's mouth latches on to my clit, sucking hard. I let out a yelp but am quickly distracted by the sticky, cool lube and then the nudge of Asher's cock at my backside.

He penetrates me, and I cry out at the burning sensation. Despite the copious amounts of lube he's used, it hurts like hell. I buck, trying to pull away, but all this does is jam my pussy harder against Wilder's face. He reaches up and grabs the backs of my thighs, his fingers digging into my flesh, holding me in place. He sucks and nips and licks my clit, and my pussy pulses in responses, flooding me with wetness. The pleasure is a strange contrast to the pain, and my body doesn't know how to respond. I'm shaking with the overwhelmingness of it all.

Asher slides deeper, stretching me around him. I've never felt anything like this before. I feel filthy and used and degraded, but it's all my own fault.

"Fuck, I'm balls deep," Asher says from over my shoulder. "You have no idea how pretty your ass looks stretched around my cock."

To think I'd thought he was the nice one when I first arrived.

To my dismay, that familiar coiling builds low in my belly. Now I've loosened up for him, his movements are easier, and he pumps back and forth, slowly, as though he's enjoying watching himself vanish inside me. My blood is burning through my veins. My pussy feels hot and swollen.

I'm like a dog in heat.

Wilder continues to lick me, and my body takes over, my hips undulating, meeting Wilder on one side of me and Asher behind. My tits bounce each time Asher thrusts into me.

Brody and Rafferty do nothing but watch, and somehow that feels worse than if they'd joined in. It feels clinical, like this is a test or a punishment, and they just want to assess how I'll do.

"Oh, God, oh, God." My fingers grip the back of the lounger tight. I know I'm going to come, and I don't want to. *I don't*. Not like this.

But I can't help myself, and utter bliss shudders through me in waves, encompassing my entire body. My toes curl, my eyes roll beneath my squeezed shut lids, and every muscle in my body contracts.

A gush of liquid floods into Wilder's mouth. Fuck. What was that? Did I just...squirt? I've always been super wet when

I orgasm, but not in that amount. I didn't think that was anything more than an old wives' tale.

"Fuck, our little Snow came hard enough to half drown me." He wipes his mouth, and I about want to die.

"I'm sorry."

"Don't be sorry. I hope you come that hard every time."

Asher pulls from my body, but he doesn't move away. Instead, he runs a finger around the stretched ring of my ass. "Gaping wide open. I bet you'll even be ready to take Wilder soon."

"No, please. No more."

He chuckles. "Don't worry. This is just the start. We want to have more fun with you before we break you."

Chapter Twenty-One
Honor

MY BODY HUMS WITH THE afterglow of my orgasm, but I'm coming down from the adrenaline high. I have nothing to wear, so, after Wilder climbs off the lounger, I hug my knees into my chest and wrap my arms around my shins.

"I'd like to go back to my room now." I feel utterly disgusted with myself. All I want is to get into the shower and scrub myself clean. Is this really better than being back on the streets and broke?

It will be if my stepfather finds me.

The men exchange a glance.

"What?" I dare to ask.

Rafferty straightens his shirt sleeves. "That room's too good for you. That's a room where women who deserve to be treated well get to go. Not you. You're a liar, and you tricked us. You put our whole business in jeopardy. We've made an agreement, but you don't get to have nice things anymore, Honor—if that's even your name."

I stare at the floor. "It is."

He cuts a glance to Brody. "I say we take her to the bunker."

A cold smile tweaks Brody's perfect lips. "I agree."

The bunker? I don't like the sound of that.

"Wilder?" I turn to the one who'd been kindest to me. "Please."

He won't even meet my eye. A muscle in his wide jaw twitches and his lips press into a line of disapproval.

I have no allies here.

"Can I at least have some clothes?" I plead.

Brody smirks. "Only when we say so."

There's no point in fighting. Wilder grabs me by the wrists and drags me out of the spa and back down the corridor. I assume they're taking me to another part of the building, but instead I find myself outside, on the grounds. The bright sunlight hurts my eyes, and despite it still being early, the rays scorch my bare skin. I pray there are no other staff around to see me like this. I don't think I've ever felt more humiliated in my life, even during the years I spent with Don Bowen.

Where are we going?

We leave the plush hotel and manicured grounds far behind us. Wilder's hold on my bicep doesn't loosen. The men surround me, Brody leading the way, Rafferty on the other side to Wilder, Asher bringing up the rear. I hop and tiptoe, trying to save my poor feet from the sticks and stones on the ground. To think I hadn't run this way because I'd been so aware of not having shoes. It didn't seem like the men cared. I hoped they were going to give me some clothes before we started our games. I wouldn't stand a chance if I was expected to run across the island completely naked. I might as well just stay put.

After ten minutes, they slow to a halt.

In front of us, steps are cut down into the rocky island. At the bottom, below us, is a solid metal door.

The bunker.

What the hell is this place? Why do they have it? This is the complete opposite of the luxury resort. It dawns on me that I've completely misjudged these men. I thought they were just in for a bit of kinky sex, but this place screams of sadism.

"What is this?" I gasp.

"This is where we bring wealthy businessmen to be tortured," Rafferty informs me. "They get a kick from it, seeing how far they can be pushed."

People come here willingly? They like to be hurt? They *pay* to be tortured?

The prospect is mindboggling to me.

Brody trots down the steps and bends to fish something from beneath a nearby rock. A key. He uses it to open the door and vanishes into the darkness.

Wilder tugs on my arm, and I'm forced to move with him. Within seconds, I've left the sunlight and greenery behind and am in an underground room. The walls are made of cinderblocks, and there are a couple of fold-out beds with thin mattresses. The bathroom is just a hose and a hole in the ground. There are rings concreted into the walls—I assume for chaining people up.

I try to convince myself that I'm still in a better position than I would be if I'd just agreed to leave. At least here, I have a bed and a roof over my head. I even have an ensuite bathroom, I try to joke with myself. No matter what, I need to stay strong. I need to own my fear and my decisions.

And most importantly of all, my stepfather can't get to me here.

One by one, the men turn to leave.

Wilder is the last, and he stops in the doorway and turns to face me.

"Get some sleep, because tomorrow you're going to be sore, terrified, and exhausted. You think you know what is coming, but you have no fucking idea." He smirks at me. "Rest up, little Snow, because tomorrow, the hunt starts for real."

About the Authors:
Marissa Farrar

Marissa Farrar has always been in love with being in love. But since she's been married for numerous years and has three young daughters, she's conducted her love affairs with multiple gorgeous men of the fictional persuasion.

An author of more than forty novels, she has been a full time author for the last ten years. She predominantly writes paranormal romance and fantasy, but has branched into contemporary fiction as well.

To stay updated on all her new Reverse Harem books, just sign up to her newsletter and grab a free short story from her Dark Codes series.

https://dl.bookfunnel.com/4t79xdwx8m

You can also find her at her facebook page, www.facebook.com/marissa.farrar.author

Join her facebook group, https://www.facebook.com/groups/1336965479667766

Or even follow her on TikTok, https://www.tiktok.com/@marissafarrarwrites

She loves to hear from readers and can be emailed at marissafarrar@hotmail.co.uk.

About the Authors:
Skye Jones

Redeeming dark and dangerous heroes one book at a time.

Skye Jones is an award winning and USA Today Bestselling Author.

She writes dark mafia and contemporary romance as SR Jones, and angsty paranormal romance as Skye.

When not writing Skye can be found reading, dog herding, or watching gritty dramas on Netflix with her husband. She lives in the grey, windswept north of England, which fuels her taste for the dramatic and the gothic.

For a free read sign up for her reader club here: https://dl.bookfunnel.com/ca20ewxx71

Printed in Great Britain
by Amazon